Panty Raid

PANTY RAID

Book 8 in the Killer Fashion Mystery Series

A Polyester Press Mystery

First published 2018

Copyright © 2021, 2018, Diane Vallere

e-ISBN: 9781954579057

print ISBN: 9781954579064

"Fashion is always at the forefront, but never at the cost of excellent writing, humorous dialogue, or a compelling story." -*Kings River Life*

"A captivating new mystery voice, Vallere has stitched together haute couture and murder in a stylish mystery. Dirty Laundry has never been so engrossing!" -Krista Davis, *New York Times* Bestselling Author of The Domestic Diva Mysteries

"Samantha Kidd is an engaging amateur sleuth." -*Mysterious Reviews*

"It keeps you at the edge of your seat. I love the description of clothes in this book...if you love fashion, pick this up!" -*Los Angeles Mamma Blog*

"Diane Vallere takes the reader through this cozy mystery with her signature wit and humor." -Mary Marks, *NY Journal of Books*

"The Samantha Kidd Mysteries continue to be completely fun and entertaining." -*Carstairs Considers*

a killer fashion mystery

Panty Raid

DIANE VALLERE

Polyester Press
READING, PA

To Amy O'Connor

1

PARIS

I EXPECTED THE EIFFEL TOWER TO BE BIGGER.

When the powers that be at Tradava, the department store where I worked, first approached me about attending the lingerie trade shows in Paris on their behalf, I said yes. After hearing the word "Paris," my mind may have gone to the land of baguettes, beatniks, and Beaujolais. Turns out they meant the trade shows in Las Vegas, not the ones in France. They booked me a room at The Left Bank, a new fake French casino that had popped up across the street from the original fake French casino (which was a fake version of Paris, France). They'd sent me to the city of sin, not the city of lights.

On the bright side, if I tired of Paris, it was only a two-block walk to New York.

Tradava was in the middle of a Chapter II reorganization after some messy details surfaced eight months ago about ties to local mafia. Considering I'd had something to do with exposing those details, I wasn't sure they still wanted me around.

But for all the bad press they received, my star was on the rise. The local newspaper ran a profile on me that got picked up by the AP wire. I was invited to sit in for a weekly stint as guest host of *Good Day, Ribbon!*, the local cable morning show. A recruiter called to see if I was interested in more lucrative positions at competitors. For the first time since I filled out an application to work for Tradava, our association was better for them than for me. Keeping me on the payroll was the best publicity Tradava could buy.

I stood on the sidewalk outside of The Left Bank while Elvis circa 1970 and Madonna circa 1991 posed in front of the half-scale Eiffel Tower across the street. The bright August sun reflected off the red, blue, and green rhinestones on Elvis's jumpsuit, calling even more attention to the selfie photo shoot than their costumes already did. Madonna smoothed her long blond ponytail, pulling it over one shoulder. I snapped a couple of pictures with my phone. Madonna reached into her cone bra and adjusted her stuffing (at least that's what I assumed she was doing). Elvis did a few karate moves with the Eiffel Tower in the background.

Ah, Vegas.

As I watched the unbridled display of attention-seeking, I wondered if perhaps the powers that be hadn't had something else in mind by sending me here. Like getting me out of town while the attention died down.

I caught a whiff of sandalwood and musk and turned around. Nick Taylor, shoe designer to the luxury market and fiancé to me, rolled our luggage onto the sidewalk. "Do you think you packed enough?" he asked.

"I packed like I was going to Paris."

"This is Las Vegas."

"Don't spoil the illusion." I grabbed the handle of my train case. "Let's get checked in."

"I hope the room's ready," he said. "We can grab some food and hit the casinos."

"Let me guess: you're a blackjack guy."

"Nope. Winning at blackjack requires too much thought."

"Yeah, um, most people like to have some control over their money."

"Not me," he said. "If I'm going to gamble, I'm going to *gamble*. Let the universe determine the outcome. Roulette. Slot machines. Craps. Win or lose based on the roll of the dice."

"Interesting," I said, studying his profile. With Nick's recent financial trouble, I'd expected him to eschew the lure of casinos. This devil-may-care attitude was a surprise.

In fact, Nick had been full of surprises recently. After his company had been tied to the mafia trouble too, he lost everything. He'd tried to keep me from getting involved, but that had backfired famously. Yet somehow, we came out of it closer than ever.

The timing of the Las Vegas trade show was

fortuitous. The past few months had been rough on Nick's business. He issued a statement to the fashion media, subleased his apartment in Milan to a friend, and put out feelers in the industry. When the opportunity to join me in Las Vegas for a few days presented itself, he jumped at the chance to get away. A luxury accessory market was taking place at the same time, so Nick would have something to do while I was busy watching models parade about in lingerie.

I would have invited him to join me, but *lingerie models*. I'm not stupid.

We entered our hotel and located the check-in desk. The room was under my name. I dug out my wallet and approached the concierge. The floor was inlaid marble with an elaborate pattern of curly waves, suns and circles. Surrounding the lobby were boutiques and restaurants, each offering the fake Parisienne experience. Baguettes and Beaujolais were still in my future. (I wasn't so sure about the beatniks.) Nick waited for me by a round gilded fountain that could have accommodated a family of eight.

"Hi, I'm Samantha Kidd," I said to the concierge. "I have a reservation for a room with an Eiffel Tower view."

"Meees Keeed," the man answered in a possibly phony French accent. His nametag said Jacques. "Welcome to Paree."

I smiled. "*Merci.*"

Jacques copied my ID and clicked the mouse. His

expression changed to confusion. He maneuvered his mouse a few times and clicked again.

"Is there a problem?"

"I'm not sure," Jacques said. "Ze computer shows all of our Eiffel Tower views are full. Perhaps I can put you in a room with a view of ze fountain?"

"I don't understand." Being slightly old-school, I'd printed my itinerary and kept it in my bag. I pulled out the folded sheets of paper and turned them toward Jacques. "I made the reservation weeks ago," I said, tapping the papers.

Jacques clicked the mouse a few more times, and then his eyes widened. "Oh," he said. "I'm sorry, Meeees Keeed. A guest of the hotel requested your room. We have upgraded you to ze French Countryside. I'll send up a bottle of our best champagne, and a voucher for fifty dollars in our casino."

I was hot. And tired. And cranky. I turned around and saw Nick chatting with a man in a gray tropical weight wool suit and a black shirt unbuttoned at the collar. The man had an expensive Goyard briefcase with the initials MR embossed in gold. Whoever he was, he had money.

And for the first time in eight months, Nick seemed completely relaxed and at ease. I didn't want to tell him there was a problem with the reservation, but I'd spent the past week watching videos people had made of their view from The Left Bank and talking up fake Paris. I'd specifically chosen this room. When Nick had suggested I get reservations at Flush, the convention center hotel where the trade shows were scheduled, I'd made a case that a Paris-themed hotel was more romantic than a hotel based on a poker hand and had promised to make our stay in fake Paris worth his while.

I was fairly sure a bottle of champagne and a fifty-dollar casino voucher wouldn't distract him from the fact that the Eiffel Tower wasn't outside our window.

I turned back to Jacques. "Would you excuse me for a moment?"

"*Absolutement,*" he said.

I approached Nick and the stranger. Nick saw me coming and held out his hand. I took it.

"This is her. Samantha Kidd. Samantha, this is Marc Rico."

Nick dropped my hand and put his arm around my shoulders.

I shook Marc's hand. "Are you in the shoe industry?" I asked.

Nick laughed. "Marc's in the media industry. He owns four cable networks and two satellite stations."

"And a lingerie company," he said.

"You own a lingerie company? Is that why you're in Vegas?" I asked.

"Not exactly," he said. His eyes were dark brown and intense. He maintained eye contact with me for slightly too long, and I looked away, embarrassed by the sense that I was being studied. I turned to look at the concierge, who was watching the three of us from the desk.

"Nice meeting you, Marc."

He smiled like I'd said something funny. Nick's hand tightened on my shoulder.

"Do you mind if I talk to Nick for a moment? Alone?"

"Be my guest. I have to check on my arrangements for tonight." He left the two of us and approached Jacques.

Nick grabbed the handles on the suitcases. "Which way to our room?"

"Hold up," I said. "Who was that guy?"

"I just introduced you. That was Marc Rico."

"How do you know him?"

"We went to college together."

I looked back at Marc. "Why did he smile when I said his name?"

"I imagine he's used to strangers calling him Mr. Rico. He probably thought it was cute."

"I don't get it. You're the same age, right? Are you used to people calling you Mr. Taylor?"

"No, but I'm not a billionaire."

"He's a bill—"

Nick clamped a hand over my mouth. "Let's talk about this after we get to our room, okay? I want to set up the iPad to take a time release video of the sun setting over the Eiffel Tower, and the light is good right now."

"We, um, don't have a room yet," I said.

"Why not?"

I pouted. "The hotel gave our room away. They offered us another room, a bottle of champagne, and a fifty-dollar casino voucher, but I...I had my heart on the Eiffel Tower view. It's stupid, I know."

Nick leaned down and whispered in my ear. "It's not stupid if it's important to you, but to be honest, I was hoping when we're in the room, we wouldn't spend all of our time looking out the window. If you know what I mean."

I did, and the mere suggestion shifted my priorities from a room with a view to a room with a bed. "I'll be right back," I said.

I reapproached the front desk. "Okay, we'll take the French Countryside room," I said, quickly adding, "and the champagne."

Marc, who'd been listening from a few feet away, stepped closer. "Put their room on my bill," he said.

"*Pardonez moi*, Monsieur Rico," Jacques said. "I did not know Meees Keeed was part of your partee."

"I'm not," I said.

At the same time, Marc said, "She is now." He glanced at my printed reservation. "You're supposed to be in a room with a view. My plans must have bumped you. Jacques, take care of them. Give them a room on my floor."

"Of course." Jacques looked embarrassed. He took the keycards he'd already coded for me, tossed them into the trash, and coded a new set. He handed them to me and set my ID, credit card, and a shiny gold poker chip with $50 embossed on the surface on the counter. "Enjoy your stay at ze Left Bank," he said. He rang a bell, and a bellman appeared with a gold-plated luggage cart.

"Thank you," I said. I turned to Marc. "I'm not sure what just happened, but thank you, too."

Marc picked up the gold poker chip, tossed it in the air, caught it, and pressed it into my hand. "Nice to meet you, Sammie." He winked and walked away.

"It's Samantha," I said to his receding back.

I shoved the poker chip into my pocket and rejoined Nick while the bellman loaded our luggage onto his cart. "Looks like we're back in business," I said. "A room with a view, right this way."

"Never underestimate your charm, Kidd."

"It wasn't my charm so much as your friend's generosity. He's the one who bumped us in the first place. When he found out we'd been inconvenienced, he fixed it so we got what we originally expected."

Nick stopped in his tracks, and I ran into him. The bellman kept walking and disappeared into an open elevator. When Nick turned around, his eyes narrowed.

"Go back to the front desk and take the other room, Kidd."

"It's already done, Nick. And the bellman is probably halfway to our room. It's fine." I forced my voice to be light and teasing. "I'll be on my best behavior and won't embarrass you around your rich friend."

"It's not you I'm worried about. I haven't seen Marc Rico since college. He's the last person in the world I want to owe."

2

POOR SALESMANSHIP

"But you acted like you were old friends," I said. "You were relaxed. And when he offered to buy us a bottle of champagne, I just assumed—"

"Hold that thought," Nick said. "We'll talk about it in the room."

We reached our room in silence. I barely noticed the touches of France the hotel designers had incorporated throughout the interior. I did notice the smell of baking bread. As soon as we straightened out this Marc Rico situation, I was going to find the location of that bakery.

Our luggage was already in the room when we arrived. The curtains had been left open. We were in one of the highest floors of the casino, and our view looked out at the top of the smaller-than-expected Eiffel Tower. I felt like Alice in Wonderland after she eats the cake that made her big.

The room was huge. It held a king-sized bed that was

dressed in eight-hundred-thread-count sheets and draped with a flaming-red throw blanket. The headboard was tufted with the same shade of red. An oval ottoman sat at the foot of the bed, and a sofa shaped like taupe lips was positioned to the right of the floor-to-ceiling windows. There was enough unused space in the room for side-by-side games of Twister or Tae Bo, depending on your preference.

Nick whistled. "This hotel was on Tradava's approved list?"

"Our original room wasn't quite this spacious, but it's a moot point now."

"Kidd—"

"Taylor." I was used to Nick calling me by my last name. When he said it, it was a term of endearment. And back when I was a shoe buyer for a luxury department store and he was one of my vendors, the familiarity of it had held a flirtatious note. "Tradava gave me a budget, and I stuck to it. Now, do you want to stand here and talk about room rates, or do you want to tell me about your friend?"

"I wouldn't call us friends."

"Paying for our room isn't something you do for a stranger," I said. "I want to know what I agreed to when I accepted this room."

I led Nick to the lips sofa and sat down. He joined me.

"What's the deal with Marc Rico?"

Nick stared at me as intensely as Marc had when we first met. I was used to having Nick stare at me—well, maybe I'd never get used to it, but I liked it. When Nick looked at me like that, I felt like I was the only person in the room. Which right now I was. (Unless someone was under the bed.) But even in a crowd, it felt like just me and him.

My heartbeat picked up, and my palms grew prickly. I could probably wait until a little later to find out what the deal was with the billionaire whose name I temporarily forgot. I traced my finger over Nick's hand and tried to remember if I was wearing good panties when there was a knock on the door.

"The luggage is already here," Nick said. His voice was husky.

I cleared my throat. "Champagne," I said. "It's probably room service."

The knocking resumed. We stood. I crossed the room and peered through the peephole. It wasn't room service. It was Marc. Already I was wondering how different things would have been if I'd stayed at the convention hotel instead of insisting on staying in fake France.

I opened the door, and Marc grinned at me. "Hey, Sammie," he said. "How's the room?"

"It's Samantha," I corrected, this time to his face. I smiled back. "The room is fine."

"Just fine?" He looked over my shoulder. "I hope it's better than fine."

"It's better than fine," I relented. "Thank you for helping us out. I'll make sure the bill is squared away at checkout."

"Honey, there's not going to be a bill. This is a celebration, and you're officially a part of it. You and Nick both."

While we stood in the doorway, the elevator bell sounded. A man in a burgundy jacket with gold buttons over black trousers pushed a cart in our direction. Before he reached us, I saw a bottle of champagne on ice and a plate of chocolate-dipped strawberries. The man slowed outside of our room. Marc pulled out a wad of bills and handed the man a twenty.

"Thanks, Fred. I'll take it from here," Marc said. He moved behind the cart and pushed it into our room.

"What are you doing?" Nick asked. He glanced at me quickly, and I sensed he was as unhappy about Marc's poor timing as I was.

"Delivering your champagne," Marc said. He pulled the bottle out of the ice, wrapped it in a red-and-white-checked towel and popped the cork. "How about a toast?"

Was this guy for real? I glanced back at Nick, wondering if he was thinking what I was.

I needn't have worried. Nick took the bottle from Marc. "Thanks for the champagne. Samantha and I would rather enjoy it alone."

Marc looked at Nick and at me and at Nick again. He took two steps back and held up his hands. "You're still mad. It's been almost twenty years, man. I thought—you and Sammie here, together, in Las Vegas—I thought you moved on."

"It's Samantha," Nick and I said at the same time.

Marc held both hands up in an I-surrender gesture, turned around, and left.

"Nick? What did he mean, he thought you'd moved on? Moved on from what?"

"It was a long time ago." He poured himself a flute of champagne and downed it. Immediately he refilled his glass.

I took the glass from him and set it on the cart. "No," I said. "You don't get to shut me out. Not while we're in Paris."

"I wouldn't bring up Paris. It's poor salesmanship."

"Don't try to make me laugh. What's the deal with that guy?"

Nick picked up the champagne flute and seemed to consider it, then returned it to the cart. "I didn't think things could get much worse after I lost the company," he said. "But this—this is worse."

My skin felt like it was on fire for completely different reasons than before. Nick lost his shoe company after his assistant had been murdered. Her death had exposed all sorts of secrets about his family. Last year, before my birthday, I'd found myself wondering how well I knew Nick. We'd been through so much since then that I believed to the center of my being that we could get through anything. Mafia. Threats against family members. Being held at gunpoint. Twice.

What could possibly be worse than all that?

"What could possibly be worse than what you've been through?" (It seemed worth asking out loud.)

He hung his head, giving me a view of his thick, curly brown hair. He pushed his hands into his pockets and looked up at me. "A woman is dead because of Marc Rico—"

My anger quickly melted into surprise and then fear. I looked at the door Marc had left through and considered the ramifications of accepting his generosity and then turned back to Nick. "We'll go to another hotel. We never have to talk to him again. But I don't understand—what does that have to do with you?"

"Let me finish. A woman is dead because of Marc Rico, but she's also dead because of me."

3

BIGGEST MYSTERY YET

"I don't believe you," I said, for no reason other than my ongoing belief that Nick was a good guy. "What happened?"

Nick didn't answer. We stood that way, staring at each other with the room service cart between us, for far too long. Nick picked up the champagne bottle again. He held it for a few seconds and then threw it at the wall. The fizzy beverage splashed out of the bottle and stained the fabric wallpaper. The bottle rolled to the foot of the lip-shaped loveseat, where what was left of it sloshed onto the carpet. I expected Nick to realize what he'd done, apologize, or offer some sort of explanation.

He turned away from me and stormed out of the room.

I was not having this. I grabbed my handbag and followed him. "Nick! Hold up!"

He climbed on an elevator, and the doors closed before I reached it.

I thought I'd already met the skeletons in Nick's closet, but this one was new—and scary. Nothing about this had come out when the rest of Nick's family secrets recently became public knowledge, which meant there were secrets about him I still didn't know. Nick was turning out to be my biggest mystery yet.

I didn't doubt he was upset. Throwing champagne bottles and leaving me at the hotel wasn't Nick behavior. Even when he'd lost his company, he found a way to deal with the ensuing outcome. Something about Marc Rico had set Nick off in a way I'd never seen, and that scared me more than whatever it was the two of them had done back in college.

I couldn't just sit around and let my imagination run wild. But I couldn't do nothing. If accepting Marc's generosity had triggered Nick's unexpected reaction, then I was turning it down. It was a lame attempt to take control of the situation, and I knew it.

Whatever memories Marc's presence had triggered in Nick, they weren't going to go away because our room was on a different floor. If being dependent on Marc's generosity had played a part in Nick's angry flare-up, then I was going to undo that generosity no matter the cost—emotional or monetary.

I rode the elevator down enough floors to make my stomach flip and approached the front desk. Jacques was still working.

"Hi," I said. "I'm Samantha Kidd."

"Yes, Meees Keeed. I remember," he said. "I trust your room is to your liking?"

"No, it's not. I would like the room you originally offered me."

"You are in your original room."

"Not the original-original room. The second original room. The French Countryside room that came with the free champagne." I thought about the champagne Nick had thrown. "But I don't need the voucher. I just want a different room." I pulled out my credit card.

Jacques clicked his keyboard keys. "We have a French Countryside room on ze sixth floor."

"I'll take it."

Jacques clicked his keys a few more times. "Ze daily rate is three hundred. Same card?"

"Three hundred? I had a room with an Eiffel Tower view for one twenty-nine!"

"That was an internet special."

I slapped my credit card on the marble counter. "Book it."

I looked around. A steady stream of people came into and out of the casino entrance. In addition to families who appeared to be on vacation, Hawaiian Elvis, in a floral shirt, white pants, and several brightly colored leis, entered the gaming floor. A family of four weighed down with matching fanny packs crowded around a map of the strip. A group of college-aged boys stood to the left, watching a bachelorette party on the right.

The women had on T-shirts that said "To-Do List: Marry Rich" next to an empty square. The tallest of the women, a curvaceous brunette with immaculate makeup, pouty lips, and boobs that defied gravity, wore a cheap white veil that one of her friends was decorating with condom packets. The bride-to-be's T-shirt had the word "Pending" written underneath "Marry Rich." A photographer stood a few feet away, assessing them through the viewfinder of a sizeable camera.

You gotta love Vegas. Total class.

While I waited for Jacques to finish with my credit card, I eavesdropped on the bride's phone conversation.

"Where are you? With who?" She ran her tongue over her teeth. "You said you wouldn't do the bachelor party thing. You promised you wouldn't get drunk. You're going to ruin everything." She was quiet for a second. "Don't bother. I'll be at work."

Yep, class all the way.

Jacques finished with my credit card and ID, and I slipped both cards back into my wallet. I handed him the two old room keys. "My fiancé left without taking his room key, so if I can't reach him, I'm guessing he'll come to you. His name is Nick Taylor. Can you make a note under his name that our room number has changed?"

"Of course," Jacques said. His fingers flew over the keyboard. What was he writing in there, the great American novel? "Will there be anything else, Meees Keeed? Would you like me to make arrangements to move your luggage?"

I hadn't thought that far ahead. "Yes. Thank you."

I slipped the new room keys into the pocket of my black capri pants and wandered the lobby. I'd half hoped to find Nick here, getting space from the immediate reminder of Marc Rico and whatever the two of them had done way back when.

I called Nick twice, but unless he'd somehow returned to the old room and charmed his way in without a key, he wasn't going to get my messages. He'd left without taking his phone. And now that I'd changed rooms, there wasn't much I could do until the bellman arrived with my luggage.

Wandering the streets of Las Vegas in search of Nick seemed a poor way to spend the first afternoon of our getaway. When I first told him about the trip, we'd agreed to spend the weekend together before our respective trade shows.

I returned to Jacques. "How far is it to Flush Casino?" I asked. It seemed as good an idea as any to register early.

"It eees over a mile. You should take ze Deuce. Are you familiar with eeet?"

"No."

He handed me a glossy map like the one the fanny pack family had and circled a few things. "Eeet eees a double-decker bus that runs up and down ze strip twenty-four hours a day. How long are you going to be heeere?"

"I'm checking out Thursday."

"Get a three-day pass. There's a five-day, but you need

seeex, so you're better off getting three and three than five and one. *Comprendre?*"

"Sure. Three and three."

He handed me a small card. "It eees twenty dollars. Would you like me to charge eeet to your room?"

"Sure."

He instructed me to walk to the Bellagio, ride two stops, and exit at my destination. "Trust me. It eees ze fastest, easiest way to get around. You'll thank me later."

I followed Jacques' instructions. The Deuce was not only convenient, it was popular. Both levels of the double-decker bus were filled with a mix of tourists, gamblers, and businesspeople. I slid into a seat by the front and arrived at the convention center seventeen minutes later. Not nearly enough time to shake my concerns over Nick.

When the news hit about Tradava's bad business practices, sales took a nosedive. At first, we hoped the trend was temporary. But as sales continued to suffer, it became clear the only way the store would survive would be to cut expenses. And the first place any retailer looks to cut expenses is at non-essential staff.

It is a horrible truth of retail that the people behind the scenes fall into this category. Shipping. Receiving. Hourly assistants. And, occasionally, buyers. It was this last category that explained why I, the lone employee of the catalog department, had been tasked to cover the lingerie shows.

My job was safe. With conditions.

Before I attempted to work for Tradava the first time, I'd spent seven years climbing the corporate ladder at Bentley's New York luxury department store as the buyer of ladies' designer shoes. Regardless of what could be said about my varied experience since moving back to my old hometown three years ago, the fact remained that I knew how to be a buyer. Tradava figured that's what they'd have me do.

Buy. For a store that was slowly going out of business. They gave me the job that I'd left behind when I chose to start over my life, and the success of the company that paid my mortgage relied on my ability to do that job.

In the past six months, I'd placed orders for chocolates, fishing gear, prom dresses, and men's socks. (I loved men's socks.) My latest assignment was intimate apparel. It was a no-brainer.

Intimate apparel runs on the highest margins in the store and works on a replenishment model. If a woman buys a 3-pack of cotton panties in size Large, the system automatically generates an order for a 3-pack of cotton panties in size Large. The goal is to never be out of stock in the basics. The only thing they needed was a person with a pulse to click "Approve" on the orders in the system. My cat Logan could have done it. (He's very smart.)

But basics were boring, and women could buy their 3-pack of cotton panties at the drug store if they wanted. There was no reason to keep reordering 3-packs of cotton panties if the inevitable result was that they'd get marked down. And marking down 3-packs of white cotton panties would mess with the high margins we needed to keep the lights on. Tradava needed something to bring people into the intimate apparel department. Something they didn't know they wanted.

Over the past six months, life had gotten so monotonous that I'd taken to wearing Days of the Week panties to keep track of time. (I lost Thursday three weeks ago, which caused all sorts of problems.) By the time I was given the intimate apparel assignment, I was ready for a change.

That change brought me to Las Vegas.

A helpful concierge and a series of small signs directed me to the Flush Convention Center. I located Registration and stood at the end of a short line. But instead of advancing, a man in a uniform came out from behind the desk and announced registration was closing early.

"You have got to be kidding," said the woman in front of me.

"This is not a joke, ma'am," said the Flush employee. "Our team was needed to remove some rowdy patrons from The Heart Club. We'll reopen tomorrow at eight a.m."

"Drunks in Vegas? That has to happen all the time."

"Sorry, ma'am. Heightened security measures."

I turned and headed back to the entrance. As I

walked, I watched a cluster of security guards escort two men who appeared to be stumbling drunk.

I'd expected to see crazy behavior in Vegas. I just hadn't expected it to be Nick.

4

BOTOX AND BOOBS

WHAT IN BLAZES WAS GOING ON? FIRST, HE WAS FRIENDS
with Marc. Then he wasn't. Now, the two of them were
practically propping each other up. I watched from the
way-too-slow glass elevator as security walked them to
the exit. As soon as the elevator opened on the ground
level, I burst out and ran toward the revolving glass doors.
I had a near-collision with a woman who entered with
the same velocity that I left with.

"Excuse me," I said.

"Watch it!" she replied rudely.

Once on the sidewalk, I looked up and down the
street for Nick and Marc. Seconds later, the rude woman
came back outside. She walked three feet ahead of me
and did the same scanning-the-sidewalk routine.

"Did you see security throw somebody out of here?"
she asked.

"Sort of," I said. "What was his name?"

She crossed her arms. "I'm not telling you his name."

She didn't have to. "It was Marc Rico, wasn't it?"

"Did they say his name? I'll sue this place. I swear. They're supposed to protect his identity when he's in their venue." She uncrossed her arms and pulled a pack of cigarettes out of her handbag. Her jacket opened, and I recognized the "Marry Rich" T-shirt with Pending written below. I looked back up at the woman's face. She was no longer wearing the condom veil, but it was the same woman I'd overheard in the lobby of The Left Bank.

The woman took a long pull on her cigarette and exhaled a stream of smoke right past my face. She looked me up and down. "You're not sniffing around him for money, are you?"

I took an immediate dislike to the woman, and not just because she didn't seem impressed with my outfit. But the fact remained—or the suspicion, at least—that this woman knew the man who'd gotten thrown out of Flush with Nick. In Vegas, that meant we were practically sisters.

I held out my hand. "I'm Samantha Kidd. Marc is with his friend, and his friend is my fiancé. That's how I know who he is. And yes, security escorted them out of the casino, and no, they did not use his name."

"What's *your* fiancé's name?"

"Nick. Nick Taylor."

"Then it's his fault tonight was ruined. Great. How do I find this Nick Taylor? I have a couple of choice words for him."

"I don't think you understood me," I said. "Nick didn't do anything. He didn't even know Marc was going to be in Vegas. We're here for the trade shows, and Nick ran into Marc in the lobby of our hotel."

"Riiiiight. And let me guess. This Nick Taylor *isn't* a businessman in need of some capital to invest in his business? Some once-successful-down-on-his-luck sob story who needs an infusion of cash to get back on his feet?"

She was right about Nick, but there was no way she could know that. There hadn't been the smallest sign of recognition when I said Nick's name. Which told me two things: her reaction had nothing to do with Nick, and Marc Rico got hit up for money on a regular basis. But her righteous indignation clashed with her T-shirt, which now appeared not to have been her most well-thought-out fashion choice.

A nagging sense that I knew this woman persisted. "You're Lydia Moss, aren't you? The lingerie model?"

"Exactly what are you implying?"

"Nothing. I work for Tradava department stores. I found your Instagram feed while doing market research. You're a strong voice in the body positive movement."

The anger faded slightly from the edges of Lydia's demeanor. She cocked her head and put her hand on her hip, opening the blazer and showing off two of the recently acquired assets. "You're a buyer?"

To maintain whatever clout that information had gotten me, I went with "yes," and not "sort of."

"I was so focused on chasing down Nick that I didn't recognize you," I said.

"I had some work done recently," she said, like we were talking about a mani/pedi and not Botox and boobs.

"Lydia, I think we got off on the wrong foot. Nick and I arrived today and ran into Marc in the lobby while we were checking in. There was a mix-up with our room—from what I overheard, Marc rented out the entire floor where I had a reservation, and when he heard the room he bumped was his old friend, Marc offered to help. I guess the guys reconnected while I was getting directions here. I didn't know where Nick went until I saw security escort the two of them out."

Lydia looked me up and down again, this time like she was assessing my credibility and not my capri pants. "You saw them? They were drunk enough to get tossed?"

"Pretty much."

"Then there's only one thing to do."

"You're right. They probably went to The Left Bank. We should head back."

"You're joking, right? I'm not Marc's mommy. I have no intention of setting that standard tonight. This is one of those equality moments." She opened the door and turned back around. "Are you coming with me?"

"Where?"

"To the bar."

I should have joined Lydia at the bar. I didn't. I was too busy trying to make sense of Nick's recent out-of-character behavior. I took the Deuce back to The Left

Bank and went to see Jacques at the front desk. "Hi," I said.

"*Bonjour.*"

"Remember the man I checked in with? Nick Taylor?"

"*Oui.*"

"Have you seen him? Did he come back to the hotel?"

"*Oui.* He and Mr. Reeeco have been enjoying Las Vegas." Jacques winked and smiled knowingly.

"Did you tell Mr. Taylor about our new room?"

He shook his head. "He and Mr. Reeeco headed upstairs together. I suspect they're enjoying the fully stocked bar in Mr. Reeeco's suite."

"What room is Mr. Rico in?"

"I am sorry, Meees Keeed. I cannot give out that information."

Fine. I already knew Marc had rented out his entire floor, and if I had to go room by room and knock on doors until I found the two of them, I would.

But first, I had to pee.

I took the elevator to the sixth floor and found my new room. The smell of smoke hit me as soon as I opened the door, and I gagged. Jacques hadn't said anything about this being a smoking room.

I used the bathroom, washed my hands, and came back out. Aside from the smell, the room was nice. Nick's and my luggage had been set on matching luggage racks. His cell phone was on the nightstand between two king-sized beds. I picked it up and checked the screen. Two missed calls and a text. All from me.

I called down to the front desk. A woman answered.

"Could I speak to Jacques, please?"

"Who? Oh, hold on." She covered the phone, but I could still hear her. "It's for you."

"Be there in a sec," I heard Jacques say in the background—without a trace of accent. I suspected the concierge was as fake as The Left Bank.

"*Bon soir*," he answered. "Theees ees Jacques."

"Are you sure it's not Inspector Clouseau?"

"Meeees Keeed," he said. "Is your new room satisfactory?"

"No, it's not. This is a smoking room, which you failed to mention. I need a different room, and I need someone to help me with my bags." I took a breath. "And I need you to update the note I left for Mr. Nick Taylor to tell him what our new room number is going to be."

"Very well. Come down to ze front desk and I'll have a new room for you when you arrive."

I returned to the lobby. Jacques was ready for me.

"You're all set. Heeere ees a new set of keys. You're in one of our most special rooms on ze seventeenth floor. Our bellman has already been notified. I've updated ze note to Mr. Taylor should he inquire about your whereabouts. Is there anything else I can do for you this evening?" He glanced at the clock behind him. "My shift is almost over."

"That's all, *Jacques*."

I checked into the third room of the day (it was fine) and unpacked. Took a shower. Read the room service menu. Twice. They purported to serve twenty-two different versions of mac and cheese, and I called down to inquire about three of them. I redressed, this time replacing my Louboutins with Tretorns. When I opened the hotel room door to go looking for Nick, I found him standing on the other side.

"I've been looking for you," he said and stumbled into the room.

"I've been looking for you, too. Where have you been? What is going on? You dropped a bombshell on me and then took off with the guy you were mad at. Help me out, Nick."

Nick ran his hand over my hair. "Kidd, I am so sorry," he said, and then he collapsed onto the bed and passed out.

5

WATER UNDER THE BRIDGE

THE NEXT MORNING, I LET NICK SLEEP WHILE I ORDERED room service. The food arrived twenty minutes later via Fred, and after signing the bill, I shook Nick awake. "Nick," I said. "Are you alive?"

He groaned and rolled over. "Water," he croaked.

I handed him a ten-dollar bottle of Perrier from the mini-fridge. He drank half. I held out two Tylenol. He swallowed them and finished the water. He handed the empty bottle back to me, and I handed him a cup of coffee from room service. He set the cup on the nightstand and rubbed his eyes with his thumb and forefinger.

"What happened last night?" I asked. "You dropped a bombshell on me about killing a woman in college and left, and the next thing I know, you and Marc Rico are being kicked out of a casino. You probably have to do something pretty bad to get booted from a casino."

"Yeah, about that..." His voice trailed off. "We talked. It's been a long time, so it was a long talk. We're good now. It's water under the bridge."

"It's not water under *my* bridge."

Nick sat up. Last night, I'd been so mad at him, I slept in the other king-sized bed. Somewhere during the night he'd stripped off his clothes, and now the covers rested at his waist. His curly hair was rumpled, and his face was scruffy from not shaving for a day. His eyes were bloodshot and puffy, the only signs of his wild night.

"Come here," he said.

"Not until you tell me what happened."

"Marc's getting married today. It's a quiet ceremony because the press would go ape over something like this. He didn't have a bachelor party planned or anything, so I bought him a couple of drinks."

"You two had more than a couple of drinks. I saw you. You were escorted out of Flush for making a scene in The Heart Club."

"Kidd..."

I moved from my bed to the edge of Nick's. "You told me a woman is dead because of you and Marc, and then you disappeared. The next time I saw you, you were drunk with the guy you claimed not to be all that close with. You threw a champagne bottle at the wall. How can you honestly think I'm going to let this go?"

"Do you want me to get into this now or after I shower?"

"Now."

Nick reached out for my hand, and I pulled away.

"I'm serious. But talk fast, because you don't smell so fresh."

Nick ran his hands back and forth through his hair a few times and then dropped his hands to the sheet. "Marc and I went to college together," he started.

"At I-FAD?"

I-FAD was the Institute of Fashion, Art, and Design. I-FAD was Pennsylvania's answer to Parsons, FIT, FIDM, and Otis. If you couldn't afford the move to New York or Los Angeles but wanted a creative background to help break into the fashion industry, I-FAD was your college. I knew several people who had attended, including Nick's maybe former girlfriend, Amanda Ries. (I'd never pinned him down on the accurate classification of their past relationship and had reached a probably-better-off-not-knowing plateau.)

"Yes. We were friends. Not best friends, but friends. He was on the business track. I was in design, but I tacked on a business major toward the end, so our paths crossed. I-FAD is predominantly a fashion school, but they have a top-notch curriculum on the business side."

"Does this"—I started tentatively—"have anything to do with Amanda?"

"Not how you think."

That wasn't no. The room was still dark since I'd chosen not to wake Nick with the flood of early morning sunlight, but the glow of the desk lamp cast unflattering shadows under his eyes. "I had a girlfriend in college. Her name was Pamela Martin. She was my first serious relationship."

I metaphorically pulled on my big girl panties (too bad they didn't come in a 3-pack).

"Pam was Amanda's roommate," he said.

"That's how you met Amanda?"

"In a roundabout way, yes." Nick took a pull on his coffee. "Marc had a thing for Pam. I knew it, and she knew it. I always suspected she liked the attention, and I was right."

"She cheated on you?"

"No, she was too honest for that. She broke up with me first, but they were inseparable within a week, so Pam didn't need a lot of time to get over me. Marc obviously didn't think there was a problem either."

Nick stared into his coffee cup, and I stared at him. Nick and I had known each other for a long time, but we didn't know much about our respective pasts. There hadn't been many serious relationships for me. My hardest breakup was when the deli counter guy and I stopped seeing each other. I had to walk an extra four blocks to get good salami after that.

I stood up and pushed the room service cart closer to the bed. Pretty sure I needed comfort food to get through this.

As if reading my thoughts, Nick looked up. "I was twenty, and life seems a whole lot different at that age. I learned a life lesson and moved on. It took a while to get over what happened, sure, but that's how it goes."

I picked up a piece of bacon and tore it in half. The crisp snap might as well have been a shotgun blast for the sound it made interrupting the silence. Nick turned to the pillow and punched it. His chest muscles rippled, and I got temporarily distracted.

"Marc gets bored easily. It's probably how he became a billionaire, because he's always taking risks and pursuing opportunities. That's how it was with Pam. He wanted her when she was with me, but after he got her, he didn't want her anymore. I watched him grow disinterested until he just moved on to someone else."

"How did Pamela take it?"

"Not well. She came to my room and begged me to take her back. She was a wreck. I'd never seen her so upset. I tried to calm her down. She spent the night on my sofa, but the next morning I told her we weren't going to get back together. I knew I wouldn't get past the way she moved on to Marc so easily, and I would always wonder if that was going to happen again." He paused for a moment. "She was found dead later that day."

"How?"

"She killed herself. Overdose on painkillers." His eyes focused on the sheet gripped between his hands. The fabric was taut, and his knuckles were white.

I put my hand on Nick's arm. "You didn't kill her," I said.

"I know that. But still, if I could do things differently, I would."

"You rejected her when she was upset, but you're not to blame." I bit my lip. "Marc's not, either. What he did was in poor taste, but Pamela made the decision. Not either of you."

"She needed someone to look out for her, and she turned to me. And my pride was too damaged to see that at the time. I wasn't there for her."

"Nick, you did what you did because it was right for you. You can't control what someone else does. You can only control yourself. Your decision speaks to your integrity, not your damaged pride. Break-ups hurt, but most people get over them with ice cream and wine. Maybe Fritos."

Nick's hand moved off the sheet and grasped my fingers. I squeezed back. As he looked at me, I saw the depths of pain that the memory caused. Nick had never spoken of that night, and I imagined he'd processed Pamela's suicide the way people work through the five stages of grief: denial, anger, bargaining, depression, and acceptance.

Or had he stalled somewhere in the process, tucked the memory deep down where it wouldn't confront him daily, and moved on? Was that why he'd been so angry that he'd thrown the champagne bottle? If Pamela was his first real relationship, then there was no way her suicide hadn't left an open wound. I hated knowing Nick carried that sadness within him, but it made him more vulnerable than just about anything I'd learned about him since we'd met.

"Take your shower," I said. "We'll talk more when you get done."

I wasn't sure exactly how much of Nick I was going to see when he threw the covers back, so I averted my eyes until the flash of Burberry boxers appeared. He crossed the room and shut the bathroom door behind him. I collected the various plates and mugs and loaded them back on the cart. I rolled the cart away from the bed and pulled the curtains open.

Sunlight streamed into the room. Sunlight that on any other day would have represented possibilities, fresh starts, and new beginnings. I looked up at the top of the Eiffel Tower, smiled, and then looked down at the base. Where the sunlight illuminated something else.

The body of Lydia Moss in her Marry Rich: Pending T-shirt, matching panties, and tacky white veil lying seventeen floors below us on the sidewalk between The Left Bank and Fake Paris. Our third room in less than a day, and this one came with a view of a body.

6

SOMETHING IN COMMON

I FEARED THE WORST. LYDIA'S FACE WAS THE COLOR OF antique lace in need of cleaning, and her body was in an awkward position. Her long chestnut hair moved with an infrequent breeze. The tacky veil lay on the ground next to her. The last time I'd seen her, she'd been angry. What had happened between last night and this morning? Nick had been so schnockered he'd passed out. Had Marc passed out too? Nick said Marc and Lydia were to be married today.

I grabbed the phone and called 911. I had my suspicions, but someone official with access to Lydia's body on the ground had to confirm it. After completing the call, I sank onto the bed with the receiver in my hand.

I forced myself to look at Lydia's body again. An ambulance parked on the sidewalk and men in white uniforms surrounded her. One stooped next to her and checked for a pulse. He looked up and shook his head.

Two others joined him and helped straighten her out and roll her onto her side while they eased a lowered gurney up next to her. Words were printed on her panties in the same font as her Marry Rich T-shirt, but I was too far away to read them. As they eased her onto the gurney, her arm fell away from her body under the blanket, and I spotted a glimpse of gold and diamond. Her engagement ring.

I immediately reached for my own engagement ring. My hands were shaking. My knees buckled, and I sat, my butt catching the edge of the lip-shaped sofa. The technicians covered her with a dark sheet. They raised the gurney and rolled it to the ambulance.

The sounds of the running water stopped. Nick was going to come out soon enough. I couldn't ignore what I'd seen, and the *oh, no* reality of Marc's future wife dying after hearing the story about Pamela Martin's death years ago made the timing awful. The bathroom door opened.

"Nick," I said. "Something horrible—outside—Lydia—"

He rushed across the room and looked down. A white towel was draped around his hips and another one around his neck.

"She's dead?" he asked.

"Yes." I took Nick's hand. "I already called the police. I'm going to call hotel security next."

He nodded and looked away from the window.

I WAS NOT unfamiliar with police procedure. By the time the police arrived at our room, I was ready for them.

With Lydia's body being part of our Left Bank room view, it was a given we would change rooms again. I packed up what I'd unpacked yesterday, emptied the coffee pot into our mugs, and wheeled the room service cart into the hallway.

At first, I considered pulling the curtains shut to block out the view, but it seemed somehow disrespectful to ignore the bride-to-be, so I left the curtains open. The ambulance had departed, but a separate team remained to establish a perimeter around where her body had been and to keep curious onlookers back. Within minutes, the biggest attraction in Las Vegas was the sidewalk. I couldn't ignore what had happened even if I wanted to.

Which I didn't. Because in one teensy, tiny, roundabout, don't-want-to-think-about-it way, Lydia and I had something in common. We were both here with men to whom we were engaged. Nick and I kept postponing the conversation about setting a date, and now, Marc and Lydia's date would never come.

There was an urgent knock on the door, followed by "Police."

I stole a peek at Nick. Technically, he was closer to the door. He was busy typing something on his phone and appeared to not even hear the knock. I left my view from the window and let the police in.

The man in front was thirtyish, with a short, military haircut and a clean-shaven face. He wore a dark-blue suit, white shirt, and a green tie printed with colorful poker chips. He was flanked by two men in dark police officer uniforms and another man in a suit with a pin that said, "The Left Bank."

"Ms. Kidd?" the man with the poker-chip tie asked.

"Yes, I'm Samantha Kidd," I said. I held the door open, and the small entourage entered.

"Detective Marbury." He held out his hand, and I shook it.

"And I'm Alain Remie, manager of The Left Bank," said the man with the hotel nametag. Beads of sweat dotted his hairline. "Ms. Kidd, The Left Bank would like to apologize for the inconvenience caused to you by this unnerving event. I've arranged for our bellman to collect your things and move you to a larger suite."

"I don't want a view of the Eiffel Tower anymore," I said.

The detective interrupted. "Mr. Remie, if you don't mind, I'd like to talk to Ms. Kidd and Mr. Taylor before you make the arrangements for their new room."

"But of course," Mr. Remie said. I briefly wondered, did French people automatically apply here, or were their applications bumped up to the top of the queue because it endorsed the hotel theme?

Detective Marbury led me across the room to the window. Outside the glass, a black curtain had been raised around the sidewalk where Lydia's body had been. The curtain blocked off the street side view first. A small van parked by the sidewalk. I stared, transfixed, while people moved about doing an efficient job of managing the crime scene.

Despite the number of people who'd arrived with him, Detective Marbury was in charge. He stood next to me, watching the workers like I had. But unlike me, Detective Marbury appeared to be emotionally detached from the scene.

"Ms. Kidd, walk me through this morning."

"Sure. I drew the curtains last night—you know, it's bright out there—and Nick came in late—"

"Nick?"

I pointed across the room to Nick, who had traded his towels for casual clothes. "Nick Taylor."

"How do you know Mr. Taylor?"

"We're engaged," I said.

I held up my left hand as if serving up evidence. Detective Marbury glanced at it and nodded.

"Nick and I had breakfast. When we finished, I opened the curtain. That's when I saw Lydia."

He looked like he expected me to say more.

"I don't know much more than that," I said truthfully.

Marbury nodded again. It was a cut-and-dried statement. He'd move on to Nick, Nick would say the same thing, and Marbury would leave.

"You called the victim Lydia. How do you know her?"

Oh, yeah, that. "I met her yesterday outside Flush Casino. I'm here to cover Intimate Mode, the lingerie trade show, for the department store where I work. You know about the trade shows, right?"

"Yes," he said.

"I went to register, and Lydia was there. She's a lingerie model."

"Do you know all of the lingerie models?" he asked.

"No, just one."

"This one?"

"Yes."

He nodded. I was starting to think he only nodded when I said something of interest. If he thought it was interesting that I knew Lydia from her modeling career, I could only imagine how interesting he'd find it that Nick was out with Lydia's fiancé last night.

Oh, no. Nick and Marc had been out drinking. Nick had stumbled home late and passed out. Marc had, no doubt, not seen Lydia because it was after midnight and it's considered bad luck for the groom to see the bride on their wedding day. I had no idea what time they were planning on tying the knot, but he might be waiting for her at the hotel chapel right this moment.

"Detective, Lydia was supposed to get married today. They kept their engagement quiet. Her fiancé probably doesn't even know where she is. His name is Marc Rico—"

"What's going on?" asked a male voice. I turned around and saw Marc in the doorway. He was dressed in a tuxedo, but the shirt was undone at the collar, and his bowtie was draped around it. He didn't look anywhere near as bad as Nick had this morning. Rich people must have good hangover cures.

"Marc," I said. "Nick. It's Marc. Detective, that's Marc. That's the fiancé."

Nick stood up. The two men stared at each other. Marc spoke first. "Guess what? You're looking at a married man."

"I thought the wedding was today? This afternoon?" Nick asked.

And just when I thought things couldn't get any worse, Marc replied, "Spontaneous decision when I got home last night. I went to her room and convinced her not to wait another minute." He grinned. "We paid off the couple in the hotel chapel and took their spot."

"Marc, do you know where your wife is now?" Nick asked.

"No. Why? She must have gotten up early to surprise me. She was gone when I woke, but that's just like her. Come on up and join us for a celebration. I've got a case of Taittinger in the tub. We need to celebrate!"

As I listened to Marc, I felt numb. How could this have happened? Who was going to tell him? I looked at Nick. Nick looked at Detective Marbury. Detective Marbury watched Marc Rico. I'd be willing to bet we were all thinking the same thing: how was it possible he didn't know?

NOSY

"Marc," I said.

Detective Marbury put out his arm to keep me from moving forward. I looked at him, and his expression silenced me.

"Mr. Marc Rico?" the detective asked.

"Yes." Marc looked around the room, at the uniformed police officers and the hotel manager. "What's going on?"

Detective Marbury spoke. "Mr. Rico, I'd like to talk to you privately."

An emotionless cloak dropped over Marc's facial expression. A normal person would have shown signs of nervousness, of a growing awareness that something bad had happened. But this wasn't a normal person. Marc was a media mogul who knew how to negotiate. He knew how to play his cards close to his chest. While he couldn't possibly be the only person in Vegas to have a good poker face, I'd bet his was in the top five.

Detective Marbury led Marc out of the room. I remained next to Nick. Again, he was checking something on his phone. I watched him study the screen and tip it at an angle that only he could see. That one tiny gesture bothered me more than Nick getting drunk with Marc last night.

Here's the thing about me. I notice things. Even when I'm not looking for them. I notice how people act around each other, when they seem to have something to hide, and when they totally aren't paying attention. You could say I'm a keen observer of human nature. Actually, you *should* say that, because it sounds better than the flat-out truth: I'm nosy. Not nosy for the sake of gossip, but for the sake of protecting people.

Nick thrust his phone into his back pocket. I touched his arm gently, and he wrapped it around me and whispered in my hair. I wrapped my arms around him and nestled my head against his chest.

"Did you know?" I asked softly. "That they were getting married last night instead of waiting for today?"

"No," Nick said. "When I left, Marc was as blotto as I was. I just assumed he went to his room and passed out. I have no idea what happened after that. I went to our original room, and when you didn't answer the door, I called down to the front desk and asked them to ring the room for me. They told me you changed rooms again."

"I'll explain about the room later," I said.

The detective came to us. "Ms. Kidd, once I go over everyone's statements, I may have some follow-up questions for you. You too, Mr. Taylor." He held out two business cards. "Here's my card. Don't hesitate to call if you remember anything pertinent."

I took both cards and handed one to Nick.

"Ms. Kidd," the detective said. "When you were with the victim yesterday, how did she seem?"

"I'd only just met her, so I don't know if I can give you an accurate description."

"First impression. Was Ms. Moss happy? Anxious? Depressed? Nervous? It was the day before her wedding. I imagine she might have felt just about every emotion there is."

"Do you mean was she suicidal?"

He nodded.

"She was...angry. She didn't know Nick—didn't know he and Marc were old friends. She thought Nick was going to hit Marc up for money, and I got the feeling she spent a lot of time protecting him from what she called sob stories."

"Is that all?"

I looked at Nick. I couldn't lie about what had happened, even if the truth made Nick look bad. "She was also mad at Marc for getting drunk the night before their wedding. She said he promised not to do the bachelor party thing, and when she saw Marc and Nick get escorted out of the bar at Flush Casino, she was furious."

He nodded. "What about you, Ms. Kidd? Were you angry at your fiancé for getting drunk last night?"

"It's not the same thing. Nick and Marc didn't expect to run into each other. They haven't seen each other for decades. Marc was the one about to get married. Nick and I haven't even set a date."

"But you had no negative reaction to the men's behavior?"

I shrugged with as much maturity as I could summon. "Nick's an adult. I trust him."

Detective Marbury nodded again. He turned away from us to leave, but not before scanning the room and pausing at the sight of the evidence—that Nick and I had slept in separate beds.

Two hours later, Nick and I were checked into our fifth room. (The fourth was a two-room suite, which the hotel no doubt considered an upgrade and a gesture to keep us from badmouthing them, but the view of the Eiffel Tower was less attractive now that I'd seen Lydia's body underneath it. I asked to be moved. Again.) This was the Napoleon Room but should have been called the Napoleon Apartment. It had a kitchen, bedroom, living room, bathroom, and lounging area. We could get lost in this place.

I unzipped my suitcase and removed a few toiletries. I wasn't going to jinx things by unpacking again.

Nick pulled out his phone and checked the screen.

"Is everything okay?" I asked.

"I'm trying to cancel the appointments I set up," he

said. He kept the phone in his palm. "How about we head down to Flush and get you registered for Intimate Mode?"

"We don't have to waste our together time on that. I'll go early tomorrow morning."

"Come on," he said, ignoring my protest.

I knew Nick didn't have that many appointments to cancel. I knew I should let it go. There were things I was going to have to accept, and I wouldn't know the intimate details of everything Nick did, but his evasive behavior was like waving a red flag in front of a bull, and Nick already knew I was a Taurus.

I'd kept in mind that we would be spending our day walking and had dressed appropriately. Today I wore a black-and-white-striped boatneck T-shirt, wide-legged white sailor pants, and lavender ballerina flats. My heels were in reserve for tomorrow. We wandered a few blocks before I sold Nick on the convenience of the Deuce. He bought a pass from Chubby Elvis (the later years) and we quickly arrived at our destination.

"Do you want to wait for me in the casino? It shouldn't take me long."

"No, I'll come with you," Nick said.

We reached Registration. The line was shorter than yesterday. Nick pulled out his phone, tapped the screen, and then looked up. "I'll wait for you in the café around the corner, okay? Take your time."

"Okay," I said. I wasn't even sure he heard both syllables based on how quickly he left.

I registered and collected my lanyard, program, and swag bag. The employees seemed to be working at peak efficiency. I wondered if the news of Lydia's death had reached the venue, and if so, what the reaction had been. I didn't want to believe it was still business as usual around the convention center, but sadly, even if they knew, Lydia's death might not be all that surprising.

After checking to make sure I had all the necessary paperwork to attend the show tomorrow, I retraced my steps to the café to meet Nick. He wasn't among the patrons. I turned around to leave and overheard a female voice.

"You have to tell her," the woman said. There was something familiar about her voice, but the speaker controlled her volume, and that made it harder to place. "You know how she gets."

"I can't tell her. Not after all we've been through. She doesn't deserve to get pulled into this."

There was no doubt in my mind that the male voice was Nick's.

And as I went behind the partition that blocked the speakers from my view, I knew exactly why I was spending so much time trying to pretend I trusted Nick while the signs indicated the opposite. The female voice was the person whose relationship to him had never been pinned down: Amanda Ries.

8

NOT WHAT YOU THINK

Nick stepped backward. "Samantha," he said.

Not "Kidd." Not "Honey." Not "This isn't what you think."

"This isn't what you think," Amanda said.

At least one of them had the decency to say it.

They're friends. They lived through a tragedy together. Nick has his own life. Their friendship isn't going to go away. The thoughts pummeled my brain while things like "did you know she was here?" and "stay away from my man!" tried to filter through.

"Somebody say something," I said. "Because I'm pretty sure you don't want me to be the one to talk first."

Amanda turned to Nick. "Tell her." She looked at me. "She might be able to help."

I turned to Nick too. Not talking was taking every ounce of energy I had, and if I opened my mouth to speak, I couldn't be held responsible for what came out.

"Amanda, give us a second, would you?" Nick said.

"Sure." She put her hand on my forearm, gave me a bittersweet smile, and left.

That reaction didn't say, "He's mine." It said, "Please understand" with a splash of "I'm sorry." If that woman was having an affair with Nick, she had audacity. I'd give her that.

I turned back to Nick. "I'm going to say three things. Number one: I trust you. Number two: I know you have a past. And number three: Amanda? That's who you turned to instead of me?"

"Kidd, sit down. This is going to take a while."

If there was one person I wished had remained in Nick's past, it was Amanda Ries. She was gorgeous and talented and, after what Nick had told me about his relationship with her roommate and the jumble of their lives in the ensuing aftermath, was in his life to stay. My jealousy of her was as unfounded as Nick's jealousy of Dante Lestes, a sometimes photographer, sometimes private investigator who occasionally popped up in my life. When I said yes to Nick's proposal, I closed the door to any possibilities with Dante. I'd expected Nick had closed his doors as well.

The difference was Nick hadn't just walked in on a conversation about secrets between me and Dante.

Nick went to the counter and came back with two cups of coffee. (I wouldn't have complained if mine had been spiked.) "How much did you hear?"

"Why don't you start at the beginning just to be safe?"

"I already told you the beginning. College. Pamela. Marc. If you check my story and you looked the whole thing up, that's what you'd read."

"I have no reason to check your story." I felt my brows draw together. "Do I?"

"My point is, I told you what everybody who knows about that situation thinks. But because Amanda and I were there, because we were closely involved, because of a whole lot of things, we've both always wondered if what everybody thinks happened is what really happened."

I blew on my coffee. Took a sip. Set the cup down. Watched Nick tap his fingers on the tabletop. Looked up and caught his root-beer-barrel brown eyes watching me. Those eyes had distracted me on more than one occasion. This time was different. This time I understood what he wasn't saying as much as what he was, and it scared me.

"You don't think Pamela killed herself, do you?"

"No," he said softly.

"You think Marc may have had something to do with her death."

He nodded.

"That's a big accusation. Can you tell me why you think that?"

He kept drumming his fingers on the table. "Pamela wasn't unstable. Not when we were dating, and not when we broke up. When she came to me the night Marc broke up with her, she was upset in a way I'd never seen. That's why I had her stay with me that night—I was worried she'd do something crazy or get into an accident, maybe that someone would take advantage of her. I knew she'd be safe at my place."

I could tell Nick had run that night over and over in his mind. He'd never mentioned it, and while memories fade in time, this one must nag at him when he least expected it.

"Tell me about Marc. How did he react to Pamela's death?"

"Marc was always driven to get started on his empire. He wasn't much of a classroom guy. He dropped out of I-FAD the month after Pamela died and made his first million within the year."

"Did you two keep in touch?"

"No. Marc's name popped up a lot at first because of his wild financial success. He was one of the original dot-com millionaires, and for a school filled with designers who needed backing, everybody wanted a way to get in touch with him."

"Lydia said something about that," I said. I looked away and searched for the memory. "When she saw you two getting escorted out of the casino, she was mad. She accused you of being the kind of friend who comes out of the woodwork to get Marc to invest in your company. I got the feeling it happened more often than not."

"It probably does, and there's nothing wrong with the practice. Part of Marc's life is investing in small businesses. Lydia may not have liked it, but that's what he does. His life wasn't going to change because they got married. It's just as possible that she wanted that money for herself."

"Maybe." I thought about Lydia in front of Flush after the men had been tossed. "She didn't act like she was in love. She was so mad that he got drunk. She said she had no intention of being his mommy. Maybe that's why they worked—because she treated him as an equal. But if she wanted a special day, it seems strange that she'd agree to a rush wedding last night. When she left me, she was headed to the bar herself. Maybe she got drunk too, and when Marc suggested a spontaneous ceremony, she thought the sooner the better? She could have woken up this morning and been Mrs. Marc Rico."

"Instead she didn't wake up at all," Nick said.

Nick was right. Something was off. If Lydia and Marc had gotten married last night, wouldn't they have followed the ceremony up the way most newlyweds did? She was a sexy, uninhibited lingerie model. There was no way physical attraction hadn't played into their relationship. I didn't know if love or money was behind Lydia's desire to marry Marc—maybe love *of* money—but a woman who marries the man she wants to marry probably wouldn't leave him alone on their wedding night. And if she did, the man would probably notice.

(I'd want Nick to notice.)

"Kidd, here's the thing. You're here to do a job. I don't want what happened to be a distraction for you."

"When the shows start tomorrow, I am going to be busy," I added.

"There's nothing you can do for Lydia."

"It's in the hands of the police."

"Right." He took my hands in his. "And if Marc had something to do with Lydia's death, then I want you as far away from him as possible."

"You too." I chewed my lip. "Except..."

"What?" Nick stared at me. His eyes were intense and his square jawline rigid. He'd taken to wearing glasses of late, and the black frames only added to the seriousness in his expression.

"Except if you're right, and if Marc had something to do with Lydia's death, then you're involved. Nick, you barely remembered what you two did last night. If anybody checks, you're going to turn up as his alibi."

9

OLD WOUNDS

As awful as it felt to say that to Nick, his lack of response told me he'd already traveled down this road and reached the same conclusion. In the ensuing silence, I reached a few curious thoughts and conclusions myself.

"That's why you've been talking to Amanda," I said. "If you say nothing and Marc was responsible, he gets away with murder. But if you speak up, you open old wounds. You told her what happened."

"I told her about Lydia."

"Does she know Lydia?"

"Kidd, I haven't been a hundred percent straight with you. Amanda is..." His voice trailed off. "Conflicted. You're going to find this next part out soon enough, so I might as well tell you. The reason Amanda is here is to work Intimate Mode."

I felt my shoulders slump. Now I had to make nice with a woman who preferred salad to pizza. "I should have known that. Why didn't I know that? I checked out the entire vendor lineup when Tradava asked me to attend. She wasn't on the website."

"It's not her collection anymore. She's acting advisor. It was all very last minute. Her new financial backer thought it would be a good idea for her to attend, so he pulled some strings."

"Don't tell me—"

"Yes. Marc now owns her company."

Amanda had been labeled one to watch in the local fashion community, but her lack of business acumen had led to decisions that just about destroyed her. I wasn't going to question this latest in a string of bad decisions, because if I shifted the lens, I could see that Amanda had probably approached Marc with this goal in mind. He was financially successful. If she were looking for a sound investor, on paper, he'd be an excellent choice. Still, if I suspected someone of murdering my college roommate, would I be able to turn to them for help?

No, I didn't wonder. I knew. The answer was no.

"There's one thing bothering me about last night," I said.

"Only one?"

I smiled. "With everything you told me, why did you go out with Marc in the first place?"

"What happened with Pamela happened a long time ago. It's entirely possible that she did commit suicide. There was a lengthy investigation, and Marc cooperated. Nobody thought he was involved except Amanda and me, and we were twenty years old and wanted someone to blame. If Marc had nothing to do with Pam's death, then he doesn't deserve to be judged. He's wildly successful and has lived with the same memories that we have. And if Amanda could get past her suspicions, then I should be able to as well."

"Okay, let's approach this like what it is. A college friend of yours was in Vegas to get married, and his wife is dead hours after the ceremony. That's tragic. If that's the truth, then we shouldn't be sitting in a café bringing up old wounds. We should be making sure Marc is okay." I stood up. "If Marc just lost the woman he loves, then he shouldn't be alone. You said yourself he doesn't have any other real friends in Vegas. Let's go find him and try to be his friends."

"You're incredible. Do you know that?" Nick said.

"I'm glad you noticed."

What I didn't tell Nick was that I needed a little more time around Marc Rico to form an opinion of my own.

———

LAS VEGAS HAD a familiarity about it even though I'd never been here before. *Casino. Lost in America. Rocky Balboa. Miss Congeniality 2.* If it weren't for all the Midwestern families with Big Gulps wandering up and down the strip, I could have pretended Mitzi Gaynor was scheduled as our evening entertainment.

A girl could dream.

We rode the Deuce to The Left Bank to drop off my registration materials. Jacques was back on concierge duty, but aside from a wave, I had no business to conduct with him. We went to our room and found Marc waiting for us. It's not every day you see a billionaire sitting in the hallway outside your (fifth) hotel room.

"Nick, Sammie, you're back," he said. He stood up and fell against Nick with a bro hug. He still wore the tuxedo he'd had on that morning, and this time the distinct scents of alcohol and body odor were present, too. The man was in bad shape.

I unlocked the room, and Nick helped Marc inside. Marc collapsed onto the lip-shaped sofa in the lounging area of the room. Immediately, he put his hand up to his face and covered his eyes. "Bright," he said. He held up the opposite hand and waved it back and forth.

"I'll close the curtains and make coffee," Nick said.

"No, you stay here. I'll take care of that."

I drew the shades, and the room went dark. Next, I brewed two cups of coffee and carried them out to the men. Marc sat on the sofa, one leg bent, his hand on his forehead and his elbow resting on his thigh. Nick sat across from him, leaning forward, his forearms propped on his own thighs. Male body language was a thing to be studied.

"Have some coffee," I said. I held a mug out to each of them. Marc waved his off.

"Drink it," Nick said. His tone suggested it wasn't negotiable.

Marc took the mug. I left, brewed a cup of hot chocolate for me, and returned. The silence was oppressive.

Marc looked up. For the first time since arriving in our room, I got a clear view of his face. He'd aged ten years in the hours since I'd last seen him. Puffy and discolored bags, swollen nose, and red-rimmed eyes spoke of his pain. "It's happening again," he said. He shook his head as if to ward off thoughts he didn't speak out loud and covered his eyes with his hand.

I looked at Nick. *What does that mean?* I mouthed. He shrugged. He seemed as in the dark as I felt.

I sat in the chair next to Nick. He shifted his mug to the right hand and reached out for my hand with his left. I held it. The small gesture reassured me that we were a team, regardless of what had happened before we'd met.

I tucked that thought away for a rainy day, just in case Nick ever asked about the deli counter guy.

Marc took a deep breath and swallowed some coffee. He set the mug on the table between us. "It's happening all over again," he repeated. "Just like with Pamela."

I felt a chill in the room. Nick dropped my hand. "What do you mean?" Nick asked.

"Lydia's death. It's wrong." It sounded like he was trying to convince himself. But as I watched the man, I couldn't deny his visible grief. He was a wreck. No amount of money in the world could bring back the woman he loved, and the loss was crushing him. "Help me, man, because I don't know how I'm going to get through this."

I couldn't just sit there while Marc suffered. "Lydia's death was horrible and untimely, but it wasn't your fault," I said.

Marc looked up. "It was as much my fault as Pamela's death was back in college." He looked from me to Nick and back to me. "Somebody's using the women in my life to destroy me."

"What do you mean? Pamela killed herself. Until the medical examiner comes back with evidence to the contrary, Lydia's death may have been suicide or an accident."

"No," Marc said, shaking his head rapidly. "The detective called. He said there are too many questions about Lydia's death to rule out murder. He's having her stomach contents analyzed, but his working theory is that somebody killed her and then staged it to look like a suicide. Somebody's making me relive what happened with Pamela."

10

A CALMING PRESENCE

Marc leaned forward and buried his head in his hands. His shoulders shook. There was no doubt he was crying. It was rare to see a man cry, especially one who'd maintained an in-charge persona since I met him, and I felt like I shouldn't be present to witness his grief. Marc's emotional torment was not for a stranger to view.

Nick stood up and pulled Marc to his feet. They hugged, this time less drunken-frat-brother and more consolation. This was the Nick I knew.

Marc pulled away and put one hand on Nick's shoulder. "You think I don't remember what happened? It haunts me every day. It's why I dropped out of I-FAD. I needed to get a clean start. I don't blame you or Amanda for not keeping in touch."

I stood up. "It sounds like you two have a lot to talk about. I'll get out of here and let you get caught up."

"No," Marc said. "You're going to be Nick's wife. There

shouldn't be secrets between married couples. I want you to hear this too."

"Are you sure?" I asked Marc while looking at Nick.

"Yes. You're a calming presence, Sammie. It'll be good to have you around."

Even Nick had the good sense to stifle his smile at that.

There was a time when Nick accused me of thriving in chaos. My best friend, Eddie, agreed. When I first moved to Ribbon from New York, I'd wanted to simplify my life, but since then, I'd been involved in one dangerous situation after another. Chaotic became the new norm, and when there was no chaos, I was off-kilter. If Marc saw me as a calming presence, then I couldn't begin to imagine what his life was like on a regular basis.

I opened the blackout curtains, and Marc ordered room service. While we waited for the food to arrive, we moved from the lounging area to the office area and sat in a small circle. Marc broke the silence.

"I met her three years ago through a private service that specialized in discreet fix-ups for men of a certain economic level."

"Is that PR for high-priced escort service?" I asked.

"Kidd!" Nick said.

"Just asking."

"Yes," Marc confirmed.

"See?"

Marc didn't seem bothered by my question. "At first it was purely physical," he continued. "She was very comfortable in her own skin, which I guess comes with the territory of being a lingerie model. The more I saw her, the more I wanted to see her, and the less I wanted anyone else to see her."

I didn't like where he was going.

"Sounds possessive," Nick said, echoing my thoughts.

"If she wanted to see other men, it would have been different. But she didn't. She quit the service but asked them not to tell me. She didn't want me to feel pressured to change our relationship. Over those six months, I got to know her on a different level. She was smart, thoughtful, artistic, and caring. She understood my world and never asked or pushed to be let in. In time I knew I wanted to make things permanent."

The Lydia he described sounded nothing like the woman I'd seen in the lobby with her bachelorettes in a Marry Rich: Pending T-shirt, or the brash, angry fiancée who'd attacked Nick's motivations for hanging out with Marc. Was it possible she'd had this endgame in mind from the beginning and simply played her cards right? For three years? And never once slipped up?

That was a lot of energy spent on the game of marrying rich.

"I wish you could have met her," he said to Nick. "You would have loved her. You too, Sammie."

I cleared my throat. "I did meet Lydia," I said. "Yesterday at Flush. I went to the convention hotel to register for the lingerie fair, and she was there. It wasn't a formal introduction, but when the two of you were escorted out of the casino, we both followed and ended up together on the curb out front."

He rubbed his eyes and looked up. "Then you know," he said. "You know she was in good spirits. She wouldn't have done this. Somebody killed her."

"About that," I said. "If you were scheduled to get married today, why'd you get married last night? Did ten or so hours make that much of a difference?"

"Come on, Sammie, you and Nick here are about to get married, too. You have to know what it's like, having wedding chapels every fifty feet, reminding you how easy it would be to make it legal. You're in love, right? I know you're both here to work, but there's got to be a part of you that's already thought it through. Heck, when I left Nick last night, he was on his way to get you so we could make it a double wedding."

I stole a glance at Nick. He said he didn't remember much from last night, and he hadn't said anything about that when he stumbled into the room. Nick glanced at me out of the corner of his eye, gave me an embarrassed half-grin, and looked back at Marc.

"Tell us what did happen last night," I said.

Nick cleared his throat. "Good idea."

Marc seemed not to notice our silent communication. "Nick and I had a lot to drink, so my memories are a little spotty. You can help me out a little, at least to the part where we woke up Lydia."

"You must have gone to her after I left. I didn't see Lydia last night," Nick said.

"Sure you did. Remember, we went into my room and had scotch. We were talking about making it a double wedding. I changed into my tux, and we went to Lydia's room to wake her up."

Nick looked at me again. This time, the smile was more of a cringe. "That's not how I remember it. I remember the scotch in your room, but everything sort of fades from there. I'm lucky I ended up on the right floor."

Marc shrugged like it was a minor detail. "We were pretty far gone. I remember waking her up and telling her I didn't want to wait a minute longer. She said her dress was with her maid of honor. I told her I needed her, not a fancy dress. She grabbed her veil, and we left."

That explained why Lydia had been in her Marry Rich: Pending T-shirt and not something classier. It explained the veil. But it still did not explain how Lydia had gone from marrying the man of her dreams to dying.

"You said something about paying off a couple in the wedding chapel so you could take their spot, right?" I asked.

"Yes."

"Do you remember anything about them?"

"No. Why?"

"I'm trying to determine the last hours of Lydia's life. Those people in the chapel would have seen her. They might have noticed something you didn't."

"I'm pretty sure those people wanted to get out of the chapel and on with their night, especially after I gave them ten thousand dollars."

"Cash?"

He nodded.

Did Marc always walk around with that much money on him, or was this trip unique? Had Lydia known about it? It stood to reason if he parted that easily with ten grand that he had far more than that available. I still didn't know what I believed about the previous night, but Marc's account of it racked up more questions than answers.

"You got married," Nick pointed out. "That means there's a chaplain or a Justice of the Peace who officiated, so to Samantha's point, there's going to be someone else who can speak to Lydia's state of mind."

"I hadn't thought about them," Marc said.

"That's good news," I added. "You need people other than yourself who know Lydia was happy about getting married. You want there to be people who saw you. You signed the guestbook, right? That's good too."

"I don't remember the guestbook. The main thing I remember was getting married in secret. I know how the press works. I wasn't going to let the vultures swoop in and ruin the moment."

"Was that a real possibility?" I asked. "I'm honestly asking. I have no idea what your life is like. Lydia said something about people constantly hitting you up for money and never knowing who you could trust. She spoke like she protected you, not the other way around."

Marc looked wistful. "Lydia was protective of me. In

the three years I knew her, she never once asked for anything that I didn't offer first."

There was a knock at the door. "Room service," I said. I'd forgotten all about it. All three of us stood, but Marc was the one who went to the door. When he opened it, a tall, thin blonde in a cropped T-shirt and cutoff jean shorts stood in the doorway.

"Oh, Marc, I just heard!" She threw her arms around the widowed billionaire and pressed her body against him in a hug that was far too familiar to be one of consolation.

11

BOPO

I RECOGNIZED THE WOMAN INSTANTLY. SHE WAS THE LITHE blonde who'd been gluing condom packets to Lydia's veil in the lobby yesterday. She kept her arms around Marc. He moved his hands to her arms and removed them from around his neck. He stepped back to increase the distance between them. "Chryssinda," he said. "How did you know where to find me?"

"Jacques told me," she said.

While the blonde spoke, Nick moved behind me and put his hands on my arms. His palms were warm against my bare skin. I pulled his arms around me and leaned back against his chest. Marc's world was complicated, filled with secrets and lies and hidden agendas and manipulations. I didn't care how much money was on the payout line. I didn't think I could survive a day in it.

Our slight movement caught the blonde's attention. "You're not alone," she said.

"These are my friends, Nick and Samantha," Marc said. I was impressed that he remembered my full name and hadn't referred to me as "Sammie the Kidd."

"Did you come here for the wedding?" Chryssinda asked.

"No, we're here for work," I said. "I'm attending Intimate Mode—"

Nick tightened his arms. I stopped talking.

"As what?" she asked. Her eyes swept me from head to toe. "Are you one of the new bopo models?"

"'Bopo?'" Nick asked.

"Body Positive. You know, real woman dimensions." She shrugged and tossed her hair. "It's a movement this season. Using fluffier models than usual."

Fluffy?

"I'm here to write orders for a small department store in Pennsylvania," I said.

"You're a buyer? Oh, that's different. I'm a model." She left Marc and went to Nick. "And what about you? Are you a lingerie buyer too?" she asked coyly.

"No," Nick said. I waited for him to acknowledge his shoe design company or pending appointments at the accessory show. He didn't.

"Nick is my fiancé," I said. He looked at me, surprised, and then draped his arm around my shoulders. I slipped my arm around his waist and rested my head against him. Message sent.

For as big as the room was, after Chryssinda's arrival it felt painfully small. Any chance for private time between me and Nick dissolved before our eyes. I knew it was greedy to think about that in light of Marc's loss, but there was something about Marc's story that didn't sit well with me. I needed time to process what I knew. I wanted to talk things out, and I wasn't sure if Nick would support that.

Chryssinda turned back to Marc. She brushed his hair away from his forehead in another act of intimacy.

"Whoever did this won't get away with it," she said. "I'll go to the press and tell them everything."

"You can't, Chryssie. You'll be busy with Intimate Mode."

"I can do both. I'll deal with the press today. Intimate Mode is open from nine to six tomorrow, but I can handle a lot over the phone. As soon as the convention center closes, I'll be back here. You won't have to be alone."

"Don't you have a PR person or a business manager to handle those details?" I asked. "Can't you hire someone?"

Marc and Chryssinda looked at each other and exchanged an unspoken thought. "This was supposed to be a private moment between two people who love each other," Marc said. "I kept it secret and made the arrangements myself. We agreed to keep it small. No family or friends or press. Just us." He looked at Chryssinda. "You have your own life. You can't monitor me twenty-four seven."

Nick spoke up. "Marc and I have a lot of catching up to do, and with Samantha busy at the show, I've got all day open. What do you say, Marc? How about I help you out?"

The billionaire looked at Nick with gratitude. "That would be great, man. Thanks."

I felt like I was observing a poker game without cards. Everyone in the room appeared to have their own motivations, and none seemed to be in sync with the others. Chryssinda was noticeably disappointed that Marc had turned down her offer and accepted Nick's, but I didn't blame him. Even if something were going on between them—a suspicion I wanted to ignore but couldn't shake—leaning too hard on the maid of honor of his recently deceased bride would have been in poor taste. And accepting Nick's spontaneous offer was the smart move. Nick hadn't known Marc was getting married. Catching up with a friend was as good a cover as any.

But Nick's motivation remained unclear. Was he being helpful? Or looking for information? Was he hoping to find out more about what had happened twenty years ago? Or was there something else I didn't know?

I pulled out my phone and checked the time. It was going on four. I slipped my phone back into my pocket, and when I looked up, Marc was watching me. "Come on, Chryssinda. Let's give these two some space," he said.

As soon as the door closed behind them, I turned to Nick. "I don't know if I'm supposed to like that guy or hate him. Help me out."

"I wish I could."

"That's it? That's your whole reaction? He showed up and acted like a broken-hearted victim, and then a lingerie model—who just happened to be the maid of honor—shows up unexpectedly to console him. That wasn't weird to you?"

"Kidd—"

"Wait. How did she know we were here? The concierge told her? Hotels don't do that. The concierge knows we know Marc, and he wouldn't tell me his room. It's against policy."

"Kidd—"

"Nick, I'm telling you, this is not good. And you're in the danger zone. Right now you're his alibi. You barely remember what you did last night. If Marc is responsible, then you're culpable. And if he didn't do anything, then whoever did something is watching you to see what you're going to do."

"Kidd—"

"What if Lydia's death had something to do with the casino? I saw the Martin Scorsese movie. I don't want to end up in a grave in the desert, Nick."

"Samantha!"

I stopped talking and looked up. Nick took my face in his hands and kissed me. It wasn't a start-your-engine kiss, but it wasn't an innocent kiss either. It may have been a shut-up kiss. Those were the ones I tended to miscategorize.

I put my hands on his chest and gently pushed him

away to make sure he knew a shut-up kiss wasn't a good lead for other bedroom activities. He rested his forehead against mine and took a couple of shallow breaths.

"I don't think you should get involved in this," he said.

"Aren't you tired of saying that?"

"I'm serious."

I forced my face into a pout. "You're always serious. And you know what? I used to believe it when you said you didn't want me to get involved, but not anymore. You're a big, fat hypocrite, Nick."

"Excuse me?" He stood up straight, but the look of incredulity on his face told me he was more surprised than angry.

"Let's cut to the chase. When the mafia got mixed up in your business, you told me to stay out of it. I thought you were staying out of it too, but we *both* got involved, and we *both* almost got killed. Have you learned nothing?"

"Have you?"

"I learned two heads are better than one."

"You learned that from *Bill & Ted's Excellent Adventure.*"

"No, that's where I learned to be excellent to each other. And that strange things are afoot at the Circle K. And that Genghis Khan had anger management issues—"

"Kidd." He leaned down and kissed the tip of my nose. "You make an interesting point."

"Okay. We're on the same page? You agree with me about this?"

"Considering everything we've heard so far, yes, I do think we might accomplish more if we work together."

This was a major relationship breakthrough! "Okay, good. We don't have a lot of time. What should we do first?"

"Well, we're finally alone, and we're engaged, and this is the last free night we have before you start working... are you thinking what I'm thinking?"

Maybe that *was* a start-your-engine kiss? "We'll have time for that later. Right now we need to do what?"

Nick had a funny smile on his face. "We need to go to the casino wedding chapel and make plans to get married."

12

THAT'S NOT BAD

"Whoa," I said (still channeling Bill & Ted). "I mean, is that what you want? To get married spontaneously in Las Vegas? While we're on a work trip? In the wake of a suicide that maybe wasn't a suicide and has suspicious similarities to the death of a woman who was romantically linked to the very same man?"

"When you put it like that..." Nick's voice trailed off. He cupped my chin and looked at me. "Marc and Lydia were supposed to get married today. They had The Left Bank chapel reserved. It seems like maybe we should go to the chapel ourselves and see if we can find the person who officiated their wedding. Maybe ask him or her a couple of questions. Together."

I blinked a couple of times. "That's not bad," I said. "Did you just come up with that?"

"No." He let go of my chin. "I got the idea earlier

today. I'd be there right now except Marc showed up, and it didn't seem like a good idea to tell him where I wanted to go."

"Do you think the same chaplain who performed their ceremony is there? If not, maybe we can somehow find the couple he paid off. That could establish a timeline, people who saw Lydia alive, her state of mind —" I headed toward the door.

Nick caught me by the arm and spun me around. "You do remember our cover story, right?"

I put my hands on both sides of his face and forced him to stare directly at me. "You just encouraged me to use our engagement as a cover story." I kissed him. "You're such a romantic."

———

THE LEFT BANK'S wedding chapel was on the mezzanine. We took a few wrong turns on our way to find it, but when we arrived, it was impossible to ignore where we were and what we could do if we wanted. Large urns of lilies filled the vestibule. Wreaths with banners that said "Congratulations!" and "Happily Ever After!" stood on easels by elaborately carved wooden doors. A row of matching bouquets sat, ready for use, on a narrow bench along the far wall.

I wasn't yet ready to examine my knee-jerk reaction when Nick suggested this course of action. I said yes to his proposal of marriage because I knew I wanted a future with him, but I still wasn't sure how to handle the whole wedding thing.

Should I invite my family to come back to Pennsylvania from California, where they'd moved when they abandoned (listed) the house where I now lived? Convince my sister to come home too? What about friends? Neighbors? Murder suspects who'd turned out to be innocent? I mean honestly, where does one draw the line when it comes to planning the guest list?

A Las Vegas wedding chapel presented an easy answer to those complicated questions.

But was I a Vegas wedding sort of woman? I'd never thought about it. And here I was, in the lobby of the wedding chapel. Where a woman dressed in a floral dress and a matching flowerpot hat, who introduced herself as Irene, just told Nick she could expedite our marriage license if we upgraded to the Gold package, and for an extra hundred dollars, she could get Elvis to stand in as a witness.

See? They don't make these decisions easy.

Even if the stars aligned and they waived the Elvis fee, I knew I couldn't do it for two reasons that I would think about later:

1. I wasn't dressed appropriately, and
2. It didn't feel right.

"What do you think, honey?" Nick asked, with his arm around my waist.

"I'm not sure," I said. "The last place we looked had those nice flower packages, and the one before that offered complimentary champagne and a discount on the honeymoon suite. It's a difficult choice."

"I'm afraid we can't offer discounts," Irene said, "but we can see if Ann-Margret is available to be your flower girl. Would that make a difference?"

This woman played hardball. "It might, but what I'd really love is some guidance." I took a deep breath, looked her straight in the eye, and asked, "Would it be possible for us to speak to the chaplain?"

It was. Irene asked us to sit outside the chapel while Chaplain Rick finished his current ceremony.

"What do you think?" Nick whispered.

"I don't know if I'm a Vegas wedding person."

"Neither do I. What I meant was, now that we're here, do you have any ideas about how to get information?"

"Aside from the meet-with-the-chaplain plan? Because that was good. *You* didn't think of that."

He grinned. "Proud of that, aren't you? Do you know what you're going to ask when he comes out?"

"You wanted to be a team. Do you expect me to do all the work?"

Nick slowly unbuttoned his jacket and held the left side open. The guestbook was nestled into the waistband of his trousers. "Is that—" I started.

"Shhh."

"When did you—"

"Shhh." He rebuttoned his jacket. "I'm going to look at it in the restroom. If Chaplain Rick comes out, start without me." He walked (awkwardly) to the door marked Men and left me alone in the vestibule.

The doors to the chapel opened, and a post-middle-aged couple came out. The woman had her hand tucked under the crook of the man's arm, and they smiled at each other in a way that could only be defined as pure happiness.

"Congratulations," I called out to them.

A solemn man in a dove-gray suit came out next.

Irene introduced us. "Chaplain Rick, this nice young lady and her gentleman friend are considering getting married here, and they have a few questions for you." She looked around. "Your man is still here, isn't he?"

"He went to the restroom," I said. "He'll be back in a moment."

Irene said something to the chaplain in a low voice, and they both looked at me. "Would you like to wait for him or get started?" Irene asked.

"We can start without him," I said. I followed Chaplain Rick into the chapel and sat next to him in a wooden pew.

"I understand you have questions about our ceremonies," he said. "I can assure you that I take my responsibilities here very seriously. To me, this is a job where I have the privilege of joining two people in holy matrimony. I witness the love they share. It's not often a job can bring you daily joy, and that makes me a lucky man."

"It sounds like you enjoy your work," I said. "I guess you see all kinds of couples. People renewing their vows, people who've dreamed of coming here to get married, and maybe even people who had a good night in the casino and get a little carried away?"

The chaplain was noticeably offended by the thought. He sat a little straighter and focused his bright-blue eyes on me in a way that suggested I was out of line. Just when I thought he was about to propose ten Hail Marys, he asked, "What are you implying?"

"Nothing! I'm sure everybody who comes in here truly believes their marriage is going to work."

I hadn't intended to insult the chaplain, but it seemed he did only see the best in each couple's intentions. In a way, it was sweet. But sweet wasn't going to tell me anything about Lydia and Marc, and while I was super proud of Nick for lifting the chapel guestbook, I was also slightly competitive, and this being the first time we'd collaborated on an investigation (my words), I had a rep to protect. In short, it was time for me to bring home the bacon.

"My fiancé's friend, Marc Rico, recommended the chapel to us. He said he was here last night, and you conducted the ceremony. Do you remember?"

Chaplain Rick's eyes narrowed. "Oh, I remember."

"Then they were here? Lydia and Marc?" I held my

breath. It seemed the chaplain could back up Marc's story.

The chaplain appeared noticeably disturbed. "I have a sixth sense about these things, and that union was troubled from the start."

13

SOMETHING ELSE IN MIND

THE WORDS LEFT ME SHAKEN. SO FAR, WHAT I KNEW WAS this: Marc claimed to have paid off a couple so he could take their spot and marry Lydia last night. The night before the two of them were scheduled to be wed. Lydia was now dead. But according to Chaplain Rick, the ceremony hadn't been a joyous occasion. I felt like I was at the blackjack table with an ace and a king and the dealer told me I had a losing hand. Something wasn't adding up.

"Can you tell me anything else you remember about last night?"

Chaplain Rick hooked his finger under his white collar, pulled it away from his neck, and swallowed. He turned his head away from the ornate floral display behind him and coughed, and then picked up a bottle of water and swallowed a gulp. "Forgive my earlier indiscretion," he said. "A wedding is between a man and a woman, or in some cases a man and a man or a woman and a woman. My role is not to judge but to make the vows official. I've seen couples come through those doors with all different sorts of motivation. I do my best to find what I believe to be each couple's truth, and that's what I speak to."

After getting a nugget of information from the chaplain, I couldn't help thinking he was holding out on me now.

"From what Marc told me— Marc's a friend, did I mention that? —he was supposed to get married today, but he and his bride were so eager, they couldn't wait. He said he paid off another couple who was here. Do you remember anything about them? The couple who originally had the chapel last night?"

Chaplain Rick smiled and patted my hand. "I get the feeling you have something else in mind with the questions you're asking and the answers you seek."

Busted again.

Before I could get out a denial or come up with a plausible cover story, he continued. "Marc seems like an attentive young man, and I'm sure it's hard to watch someone you care about become betrothed to another. The right man is out there." He smiled sweetly. "Trust that there is a master plan for you, Samantha."

"I don't—I mean, Marc and I—I mean—my fiancé is outside. He's—he's in the restroom."

"Oh?"

"Kidd?"

I whipped my head around. Nick entered the chapel and approached us. Seeing my alarmed face, he put his hands on my shoulders. I put my hand on top of his and squeezed and smiled at Chaplain Rick.

"This is him."

The chaplain looked back and forth between our faces as if looking for any indications we were lying. I put my left hand—the one with my engagement ring—on top of my right hand on top of Nick's hand. A small cramp seized up on my right side from the unnatural twist of my torso, but the pain seemed necessary.

"Are you feeling better, honey?" I asked Nick.

Nick looked confused. "Um, sure."

I turned back to the chaplain. "Nervous stomach," I said.

Nick's arm tensed. I looked back at his face and saw a forced smile.

The chaplain's smile returned. "It happens. Trust me when I say true love does not have to be rushed. If it's meant to be, young man, you'll get over your nerves and be ready to say 'I do' in no time."

"I'm sure you're right, Chaplain," Nick said. "There is something about this one that makes me feel things I've never felt before."

"Well, if the feelings persist, you can always take Kaopectate."

______

OUR TRIP TO the chapel had been worthwhile. The chatty chaplain had confirmed that the circumstances of Marc and Lydia's spontaneous wedding weren't as idyllic as he'd like us to think. I couldn't wait to tell Nick, but even more so, I was eager to learn what he'd discovered from the wedding guestbook. When we stood up to leave, I wrapped my arm around his waist. He stiffened and stepped away.

Irene noticed and called me to her. "Don't force things, honey. He'll come around."

"Thank you for your advice," I said and followed Nick out.

Being guests of a casino hotel meant a certain amount of white noise surrounded us at all times. When we'd first walked through, buzzers, bells, laughter, and cheers had assaulted my hearing. We'd been here for twenty-four hours, and already the sounds were fading into the background as part of the experience of Las Vegas, like taxicab horns in New York and wind in Chicago.

Nick walked ahead of me, and any conversation we were going to have was squelched for now. I was surprised he could move that fast with a guestbook tucked into the waistband of his trousers. Nick had hidden talents.

We went down the stairs from the mezzanine to the main floor and passed the giant slot machine by the entrance of the casino floor and the boulangerie that opened onto the lobby. My stomach growled. It seemed like forever since we had eaten, and I wasn't exactly the type to skip a meal. When Nick jabbed the Up button by the elevator, it occurred to me that the reason he was walking so fast maybe had nothing to do with the guestbook in his waistband.

"Are you annoyed with me?" I asked.

"Should I be?"

"I don't know. Did you find something out in the guestbook?"

"Forget the guestbook. It was a bad idea."

"Why? Oh. You feel guilty."

"I don't feel guilty. I just don't want to talk about it here."

"But it was your idea, Nick."

"Not now, Kidd."

He didn't say anything until we reached our room. I was boiling hot by that point and pretty sure we'd be sleeping in separate beds again.

"This isn't fair, Nick. That whole thing was your idea. You brought it up to me. We're supposed to be spending time together, so if that's what you wanted to do then I'll do it, but you don't get to flip-flop on whether or not we should ask questions about what happened. Tomorrow morning, I have to go to the lingerie show. I'll be at Flush until five o'clock, and I can't sleuth from a room filled with lingerie models."

Nick grabbed my wrists and kept my arms by my sides. His eyes were dark, and his face was intense. "I just lifted the guestbook from a wedding chapel. Do you want to know why? Because that's what I thought you would do. I was locked in a bathroom stall with a stolen wedding chapel guestbook outside of the place where couples proclaim their love to each other because I asked myself, 'What would Samantha do?'"

That sounded romantic if you took away the whole bathroom stall thing.

"There I was, with the guestbook propped on the tank of a public toilet that a chaplain now thinks I needed because the thought of marrying you gives me a nervous stomach."

Okay, that took a little more of the romance out of it. But still, none of my dates ever asked themselves "What would Samantha do?" Not even the deli guy.

I chewed my lower lip. I could tell I was expected to say something here, but there's a delicate line between apologizing for being me and asking Nick to, in the future, keep mention of public bathrooms out of his romantic conversations.

"Is this about my bad decisions?"

Nick pulled the guestbook out from under his jacket. He slammed the book onto the corner of the bed and pointed to it. "This is about the fact that I just risked a bolt of lightning for stealing from a chapel because when I looked at things like you do, I thought it would tell us something."

"Geez, Nick! I didn't expect you to steal it! I thought maybe you'd take a picture of the page with your phone and then slip the book back on the counter while I distracted Irene by asking where she bought her hat."

"That's what I was going to do," he said. He opened the book and flipped through several pages until he reached the most current. "Except there's one problem."

"What?"

"The page we want is missing. Any details that were in here last night are gone."

14

TOO EASY

IT WASN'T SO MUCH THAT I DIDN'T TRUST NICK, BUT THAT I had to see with my own eyes to process the information. I flipped a few pages back, and a few pages forward, and then held the book upside down and shook it so anything tucked between the pages would fall. Nothing did. The most recent entry was for today, slightly before the time Nick and I had arrived at the chapel. The page before that one had been removed.

Wedding guestbooks are often bound with a saddle stitch which lends them an heirloom quality. This one was no different. When the page was torn from the book, the corresponding half of that sheet of paper remained behind. The same thing happened when you ripped a page out of a composition book, which I'd learned when I was going through my *Harriet the Spy* phase at ten years old. I always knew *Harriet the Spy* was a good influence.

I laid the book down and flipped through the pages a

few more times and then shook the book again. Two pieces of paper were loose. I pinched the edges of each and slowly tugged so they stuck out from the even edges of the still-bound pages. Taking extra care not to damage the binding, I located the loose page and slowly found the spot where the corresponding half would be. One was the page before today's page. No surprise. Nick had already told me that page was missing.

What surprised me was the *other* missing page. The one in front of the one we wanted. Based on what we knew, I found it suspicious enough that one page had been removed. But two? What else had been in that book?

When I finished examining the guestbook, I closed the cover and sat on the bed next to it. "I know you took a risk to get that, and as far as I'm concerned, it was a good idea. We'll figure out a way to get it back to the chapel."

Nick lowered himself next to me. "You just figured out that a second page was removed from the book, didn't you?"

I nodded.

"That never occurred to me."

"It doesn't matter. We don't know what was on the first page or if it has anything to do with the second page. It doesn't matter if we find out something, only if we find out something relative to the problem we're trying to solve." I was so busy trying to figure out our next move that I didn't realize Nick was staring at me. "What?" I asked.

"You don't usually talk like that around me," he said.

"I know you don't like this part of my life. I try to keep it hidden as much as I can."

"Kidd, I like every part of your life."

"Yes, but you have your things, and I have my things, and I know that, and it's probably best if it stays that way."

"Who told you that?"

"I don't know. I probably learned it from a Go-Go's song."

"Yes, I have my 'things' as you put it. And yes, you have your 'things.' But I want to build a life with you, and that means accepting everything about you. Not just accepting it. Cherishing it." He brushed a strand of my dark hair away from my face. "You accepted when my dad moved in with me. You accepted the truth about my family and my business. You put your life on the line. You have to believe I'd do the same thing for you if it came to that."

"You have," I said. "You've been there for me more than once. You saved my life with a shoe. Remember? Just like Prince Charming."

"I don't remember Cinderella being in an interrogation room when Prince Charming showed up with the glass slipper."

"You know what I mean." I shifted my position on the bed to face him. "Nick, I figure things out because I can. When things don't fit, I keep on working at them until they do. It's like one of those standardized tests, where you stare at pictures to find a pattern. I love those things."

"Nobody loves standardized tests."

"I do. You know when I moved back to Ribbon I had a hard time, right?"

He nodded.

"I was like a bull, just plowing ahead into every crazy situation. I didn't even know enough to be afraid half the time. But that's because even though my personal life was a mess, I could concentrate on the other problems. I knew something didn't fit, and I knew if I studied the situation long enough, I'd figure it out."

"Is it possible we could solve this whole interest in crime by getting you a thousand-piece jigsaw puzzle?"

"Too easy."

———

MONDAY MORNING, I woke to my alarm. We'd spent the balance of last night with adult activities that kept us in the same bed before taking a joint shower, ending up in the other bed for round two, and snuggling up to sleep.

What I didn't tell Nick was that I had a plan. Lydia and Chryssinda were lingerie models, and I was going to spend the next three days at the lingerie fair. While Nick helped Marc with whatever details had to be attended to, I'd see what I could find out about the two models' lives. With the perfectly sound cover story of representing Tradava, I'd have unrestricted snooping access to their world. If they had friends, I'd make them my friends. If they had enemies, I'd find them, too.

I dressed in a strapless pink top and long, narrow pencil skirt, added a collarless black blazer, and black sandals that laced up to mid-calf. Despite the weather report of highs in the eighties, it was hard to predict the climate of the convention center. I doubted it would be cold since the models would be in barely any clothes. But still, layers felt appropriate.

By now, I had the Deuce down to a science. I left The Left Bank, arrived at the Bellagio, and climbed aboard the double-decker bus a few minutes later. In record time, I was back at Flush Casino. A couple of elevator rides and a brief check-in at Registration, and I was ready to go.

Entering a convention center in full trade-show mode is something like discovering the underwater city of Naboo. Once through the doors, there was a whole world that outsiders knew nothing about. Over five hundred thousand square feet of convention center space had been divided into booths with elaborate pipe-and-drape configurations. This being a show for the intimate apparel industry, platforms for models, changing areas, secluded screening rooms, and displays of raw materials to be ordered for private label production were necessary, as was a back-corner runway for trend presentations.

In addition to the vendor booths and sales representatives, models in underwear walked about, loosely covered in long, open robes. One might have thought the proximity to showgirls on the Vegas strip would desensitize me to the presence of mostly naked women. It did not. What it did was make me:

1. Regret the six pieces of bacon I had with breakfast, and
2. Happy I'd worked off some calories before (and after) breakfast, and
3. Thankful I hadn't asked Nick to join me today.

There's only so much one can expect from a fiancé.

I consulted my agenda. My first appointment was with Joey Cheeks, a new-to-me designer whose collection appeared interesting for Tradava's client base. I found his location on my convention center map (Blue section), checked it against a giant blown-up floor plan by the front wall, and headed that way. I passed two models in cotton panties and cropped T-shirts. One T-shirt said, "Taken." The other said, "I'm with her."

There was something familiar about their T-shirts, and it took me a moment to realize they were similar in style to Lydia's "Marry Rich: Pending" one. As the models passed me, I turned around. Both women had #GetCheeky printed across their fannies.

The memory of Lydia's body on the sidewalk came back to me. I'd recognized her from her T-shirt and veil, but there had been something printed across her panties as well. It was going to be hard to give the designer the proper level of professionalism with that memory burned into my brain.

That turned out not to matter. As I got closer to Joey Cheeks' booth, I heard a male voice addressing his staff.

"I went to great lengths to get publicity for the collection. Six months from now our panties are going to be on every ass in the country."

"I guess it takes an ass to dress an ass," said a voice next to me.

I turned and saw the two models who'd passed me earlier. The other one giggled.

I inched closer to the booth and strained to hear the conversation inside. "But Lydia isn't here yet," said a woman with a New York accent.

The man swore. "This is exactly what happens when models get famous. They think they can live by their own rules. Was it an 'I'm running late' excuse or a 'you'll get me when you get me' excuse?"

"Neither. Nobody's heard from her."

The man cursed again. "I can't believe I signed her for a two-year exclusive contract. Teresa, call the lawyers. Tell them to find me a loophole. Lydia is out."

"What about today? I doubt I'll find a fill-in model on such short notice. Not with Lydia's portfolio. She's the hottest model at the show."

"I can't build an empire with irresponsible models and employees. Call the agency."

"I'll see what I can do."

Two thoughts jabbed my brain like the index fingers of a five-year-old who just discovered an unattended piano. One had to do with Lydia's recent and possibly yet-to-hit-the-news demise. The other included words like "suspect" and "motive."

My head hurt with dueling thoughts. Just as I pulled out my cell phone to call the police, the soft pink curtain pulled open, and a man with a shiny black pompadour, long sideburns, and chrome aviator sunglasses glared at me.

"This is a private booth," he snarled. "If you so much as think about using what you know from spying on me, I'll call security and have you tossed from the trade show."

There was no mistaking the voice as that of the speaker who'd complained about Lydia's absence. What I didn't know was what he expected me to do.

15

CHEEKY PANTIES

COVER STORY. WHAT WAS MY COVER STORY? OH, YES. THE truth.

"I'm Samantha Kidd. With Tradava department stores. I have an appointment to see the collection." I stepped backward and looked up at the logo. "This is Cheeky Panties, isn't it? I'm a little early, but I hoped that wouldn't be a problem." As confident as I was that my agenda had been set before I left Ribbon, I let my statement turn into a question.

"You're here to view the collection," he said. His eyes narrowed behind his red-lensed glasses. "You're a buyer?"

"Yes." Ish.

He turned around and knocked on the melamine table inside the booth. "Teresa, I thought you canceled all my appointments this morning?"

A petite woman with streaked strawberry-blond hair

secured in a low side ponytail came out from behind the curtain. She wore an olive-green satin bomber jacket over a T-shirt that said #GirlBoss, and ivory knit jog pants with elastic cuffs. What she lacked in genetic height she made up for in neon-pink stiletto-heeled pumps that were unexpectedly large for her otherwise small frame.

"I canceled all the appointments but one. I didn't have a way to reach Samantha Kidd from Tradava."

The man looked at me. The woman looked at me. I held up my lanyard. SAMANTHA KIDD. TRADAVA.

"Samantha, hi!" the woman said. Immediately I placed the New York accent I'd heard earlier. "I'm Teresa Kander, Joey's line manager. Sorry about the mix-up. Come on in." She unclipped the pink velvet stanchion and stepped back so I could enter the booth. After the initial drama, it felt a little like gaining entry to Oz.

Everything about the man's attitude shifted. "Samantha Kidd from Tradava. Where is Tradava? New York?"

"Pennsylvania."

"Philly or Pittsburgh?"

"Philly side."

"Cheesesteaks?"

"Pretzels."

He held out his hand. "I'm Joey Cheeks."

We shook hands. Teresa clipped the stanchion closed behind me.

"Teresa, get me a set of line sheets, an espresso, and"

—he turned to me—"you want anything? Yes. You want an espresso too. Trust me." He turned back toward Teresa. "Two espressos and get a couple of Diet Cokes for the models while you're at it. I'm taking Samantha Kidd from Tradava to the display."

"Sure thing. Be right back." Teresa sprang into action like she was wearing Nikes. I admired her efficiency. Maybe it was the track pants.

Joey Cheeks looked like he'd stepped out of the pages of a Fifties pretty boy men's magazine. If his hair wasn't naturally black, there were no traces of its natural shade. He'd dyed it shoe-polish black and styled it with a product that gave it a sheen. While there was no doubt Elvis was his spirit animal, his outfit, a white T-shirt, dark blue jeans, and red windbreaker, had been lifted from another icon: James Dean in *Rebel Without A Cause.*

"Please forgive me for my reaction back there. Shows like this are great for exposure, networking, and convenience for the buyers, but it seems we designers spend every minute playing keep away from knock-off artists."

"You thought I was trying to steal your designs?"

"Happens all the time. Sometimes they have inside help."

"Your employees?"

"The models," he said with disdain.

I followed Joey Cheeks behind a fabric partition that separated his samples from the prying eyes of people who'd gained entrance to the show for reasons other than placing orders and ogling half-naked women.

Gaining attendance to Intimate Mode hadn't been difficult, but that was because I legitimately worked for a store that carried intimate apparel. Even with Tradava's financial problems, it was a five-store chain that needed merchandise to sell. That was five times the order a small boutique would place. But I wondered how hard it would be for someone to fake credentials, shop the market, and source raw materials and production? Knowing how quickly knockoffs showed up in the market, it had to happen more often than not.

It was obviously a real concern for Joey, but it made me think along other lines. If Lydia's murder wasn't connected to Marc, could it have been related to either her job or one of her escort clients?

If her modeling career continued on its current trajectory, it wouldn't be long until she crossed into supermodel territory. That would bring professional jealousies and backstabbing to a whole other level. Plus, she'd have behind-the-scenes access to designer collections before the public, and that information could prove valuable to the knockoff market. And if not her job, were there possessive former escort clients who didn't want Marc to take her off the market? Or someone who feared she'd reveal his identity?

Jealousy. Theft of intellectual property. Fear of public humiliation. I'd found three possible motives for murder before my first cup of coffee.

Behind the curtain were bright chrome rolling rods holding T-shirts and panty samples. A floor-to-ceiling display of framed cotton displayed messages: *BIG GUNS, BORN THIS WAY, BAD GIRLS MAKE GOOD GIRLFRIENDS, BOTTOMS UP,* and the one I'd seen on Lydia: *TO DO: MARRY RICH: Pending.* At the time, I thought she'd written "Pending" on herself, but by the looks of the display, that was how the T-shirt was produced. Across the top of the frame were the words Get Cheeky!

"These are yours?" I asked Joey.

"That's right. Cheeky Designs. Get it? Ironic underwear with just enough crass to turn heads."

"I think I saw your designs on a bachelorette party last night. At The Left Bank?" I pointed to Marry Rich. "I'm pretty sure I saw this one on Lydia Moss."

A flush of color washed Joey's face, and his mouth drew into a narrow line. "Lydia Moss is our new company spokesmodel, so yes, she does have access to the samples."

"She was probably trying to do her job. Get you some publicity. I'm not up on the emerging models in the industry, but everybody's trying to grow their platforms through social media. She was no different. That's why you hired her, right?"

Joey curled one lip and peered at me over the top of his Elvis glasses. "Samantha Kidd from Tradava, how long have you been in the industry?"

"You could say I've been in women's lingerie since I graduated from my training bra," I said, hoping to avoid the actual answer, which was more along the lines of "since I registered twenty-seven minutes ago."

Joey accepted my answer with a laugh.

Whatever it was that Joey Cheeks had been fired up about five minutes ago, he quickly transitioned into enigmatic and slightly butt-kissing designer. It was a character I was first exposed to in my days working for Bentley's New York.

Faking friendships with my vendors had been among the more uncomfortable aspects of my job. It required a bit of politicking, maintaining positive relationships so my store could have leverage when it came time to negotiate. I'd had my share of vendor dinners, tickets to shows, swag bags, and complimentary samples up to a value acceptable by my employer.

Over countless market weeks, I'd learned which vendors drank too much, gossiped too much, and generally expected too much. I'd learned to blame my company when offered inappropriate presents. I learned to order the second least expensive entrée on the menu so as not to appear cheap but also not incur unnecessary debts. In the seven years that I'd held that job, I booked fewer and fewer social engagements. By the time I quit, the only invitations I accepted with any regularity were those from Nick.

We never crossed the line.

But all that knowledge of designers and vendor reps had provided an insight into the personality that stood before me. When Joey Cheeks looked at me he saw one thing: a buyer with the budget to place an order. Joey Cheeks was going to tell me anything I wanted to know.

Which brought me to an interesting observation. Joey wanted me to write orders for him. From what I'd overheard, he wanted big orders. In light of Lydia's death, his mention of publicity had shaken me, because it was too selfish of a thought. But I didn't know if Joey knew about Lydia. Joey didn't act like a man who had just learned the face (body) of his company was dead. His comments about Lydia's absence had been about the impact her actions would have on him.

Unless he knew and was pretending he didn't.

There was no way Lydia would have had samples of Joey's collection for her bridesmaids if he wasn't aware of it—unless Joey trusted his line manager, Teresa, completely and let her make the decisions. But so far, I'd seen a hands-on company owner who had his finger in every pie. If this man was responsible for Lydia's death to get a publicity, then he was truly diabolical. Especially if he'd done all that twelve hours ago and was here, at Intimate Mode, promoting his collection of panties.

Joey kept up the charming act as he walked me around his booth, but try as I might, I had a hard time warming up to him. Apparently, I did a poor job hiding my thoughts.

"You heard me talking with my line manager about

Lydia, didn't you?" Joey said, pausing the TV that had his runway presentation running on a loop.

"I may have caught a word or two."

He sat back. "Signing Lydia was a coup—at least I thought it was—but she's caused problem after problem since before the ink was dry on her contract. I threatened to cancel it, and she said she'd sue the pants off me. Have you ever had to deal with a problem employee?"

"Sure." I shrugged. "Workplace drama comes with the territory." At his confused look, I clarified, "If you work alone, you'll probably love your staff. If you work with others, it's just a matter of time until there's a personality clash."

"At this point, I'm trying to make the best of a bad situation. Maybe you're right. Maybe Lydia managed to get me some publicity after all."

Joey was either the most calculating and detached designer I'd ever met, or he didn't know about Lydia. I waffled on whether to blurt it out, but the longer we chatted, the more awkward the news (coming from me) would be.

The curtain that kept us separated from the prying eyes of the public pulled aside, and Teresa interrupted us. Her side ponytail had come slightly undone, and tendrils of hair hung loose on the opposite side of her head. "Have you seen this?" she asked Joey. She held up a newspaper. The image was Lydia Moss's body on the sidewalk in front of the Eiffel Tower with the words

#GetCheeky printed across her butt. "Lydia Moss killed herself last night."

Joey grabbed the newspaper and scanned the article. "She's gone? For good?"

"That's how it seems," Teresa said.

Joey stood up and thrust the newspaper back at her. "At least she showed them her good side."

16

A CONTENTIOUS RELATIONSHIP

I stared, horrified, at Joey's back as he left the booth. He'd made no secret of his regret over signing Lydia, but to make such a callous comment after seeing a picture of her dead body was chilling.

"He didn't mean that," Teresa said. She set a cardboard drink holder on the table and placed one of the take-out cups in front of me and another on the table in front of the chair Joey had vacated. The third cup had a straw with a ring of lipstick that matched Teresa's own. She pulled that cup out and tossed the cup holder into the trash like a Frisbee. "Joey and Lydia had a contentious relationship since the beginning, but deep down he loved her. He loves them all. That's why he got into this business."

She pulled a Diet Coke out of the pocket of her bomber jacket and popped the top. She removed the lid from the third cup and dumped the cola inside then swirled it a few times and snapped the lid back into place. I pulled the lid off my espresso and sniffed it. It smelled bitter. I looked longingly at Teresa's soda.

She held up her index finger. "I'll be right back." She pushed the curtains open, and the breeze left in her wake caught the newspaper and blew it from within my reach to the floor next to the chair in front of me.

The news of Lydia's death was out, and I wanted to know what the press had said. I had no idea how long my window of alone time would last, so I acted fast. I slid down in my chair and used the tip of my heel to drag the newspaper toward me. When the newspaper was within reaching distance, I bent down and picked it up.

Whoever had taken Lydia's picture had done so without authorization. I reached that conclusion because I'd been there. I'd been the one to call the police. As soon as the police and EMTs arrived, they'd checked her pulse and then moved her onto a gurney, covered her, and placed her into the ambulance. Additional staff had screened off the sidewalk.

That told me a few things: someone else had seen Lydia's body and had not only done nothing to help her, they'd taken a tasteless picture and profited by selling it. It did not escape me that the only identifiable thing about Lydia in the photo was the #GetCheeky slogan written across her panties. I guess that told me a third thing: someone thought it was more important to capture that angle than her face.

I doubted it would be difficult to find a copy of the

newspaper once I left the trade show, so after scanning the article, I pushed it aside. The unidentified staff writer had provided the briefest of details: *Longtime Las Vegas resident Lydia Moss, lingerie model and face of Cheeky Panties, was found dead outside The Left Bank early Sunday morning. Initial rumors of suicide have not been confirmed by the medical examiner.*

Distracted by my thoughts about how to find out who took the photo, I jumped when the curtain pulled open. Teresa was back. She'd taken off her satin bomber jacket, and her #GirlBoss T-shirt was prominently displayed.

"Sorry about that," she said. Her eyes jumped from me to the newspaper. She moved it a few inches away from me, folded it, and tucked it under her arm. She opened the top drawer of the file cabinet.

For an awkward moment, she stared inside at the contents as if she'd completely forgotten why she opened it. She cut her eyes to me, saw me watching her, and shifted her position to block my view. When she turned around, she held a packet of line sheets and sample photos. The newspaper was nowhere to be seen. I assumed she put it in the drawer.

"It's been a crazy morning," Teresa said.

"That article—that's horrible. Will Joey be okay? He said he recently signed Lydia to work for him."

"Joey will land on his feet. He always does." She glanced inside the drawer again and then slammed it shut.

We conducted our appointment like nothing unusual

had happened. I flipped through the rack of samples. The tasteless T-shirts were parsley—they could have been made by any vendor in America and would have done far better in the juniors' department than intimate apparel. It was clear Joey had outsourced the production of those designs and cared little about them, and when Teresa moved the rack of samples out of the way, I understood why.

Joey Cheeks was angling to be the panty king of the universe.

Displayed on tables shaped like white wedding cakes with Get Cheeky! signs on top were mountains of colorful panties. Hundreds. There were cotton panties, lace panties, silk panties, and even Days of the Week panties. Thongs, briefs, bikinis, Brazilians. Boy shorts and G-strings. Every pair of panties had a hang tag that said: *Bet your bottom dollar on Cheeky panties!*

I had to give him credit for the pun.

"What do you think?" Teresa asked.

"I think Joey's passionate about panties."

She laughed. "He took lemons and made lemonade, that's for sure."

"What do you mean?"

She shrugged. "Joey's had a hard life. Got bullied for being...different. It was touch and go there for a while, but when he got the idea to use his name for the panty collection, everything came together. These days he's a whole different person."

THERE ARE A few skills needed to be a successful

buyer. One is a taste level. Being able to peruse merchandise and know what was appropriate for your customers and what wouldn't resonate with them. It wasn't enough to place orders to suit a buyer's personal tastes because that was far too narrow of an audience. One customer, no matter how good they were, could not save a season, especially if that one customer flexed an employee discount. No, a buyer needed to understand the big picture patterns of the store's customer: the needs she had in terms of drawer space, personal beautification, and feel-good, emotional desires.

It was usually the emotional need that made the difference between an okay-selling item and a runaway bestseller, and emotional needs were created by buzz. It had happened in the lingerie business once before.

The intimate apparel industry had seen unprecedented growth in the Madonna days of the eighties. After the pop star's various innerwear-as-outerwear outfits showed up on MTV, bras and bustiers weren't just about engineering. They were fashion.

Joey Cheeks wasn't in the business of intimate apparel. Joey Cheeks was in the business of fashion. A trade show would generate the usual orders, possibly pick up a few new accounts. For Joey's line to transcend his industry, he needed something big. Something eye-catching. Something that would make everybody talk about his product.

A dead lingerie model photographed in his product would fit that bill.

This morning, everything I'd learned pointed to a replay of Marc's past. I'd come to Intimate Mode to get away from my suspicions, and now I was face to face with brand-new ones.

I selected an assortment of panties for Tradava and made notes on my line sheets. Between refills of Diet Coke, Teresa re-ponytailed her hair and held the samples while I photographed them. We recapped size availability, color swatches, and discount terms, and I asked about exclusives like a good buyer. I told her I'd write up the order and be in touch.

Teresa, pleased with the promise of business, excused herself again and went to the front of the booth. I had no intention of writing up the order, at least not until I knew more about Joey Cheeks. Because despite the fact that he trafficked in underwear, I'd bet *my* bottom dollar he was hiding something. But what?

As I scanned my surroundings, I heard two hushed female voices talking out front.

"Lydia's dead. Joey told me he was going to get her out of the picture, and now she's dead. He was at The Left Bank last night. He dropped off the samples. He was there, don't you see?"

"You don't think Joey did this, do you?"

I recognized that voice as Teresa. I stood up and inched closer to the curtain, hoping to identify the other speaker.

"You saw how mad he was when he found out about her past," said the first voice.

I peeked through a sliver of space between the curtains and recognized Chryssinda.

"When Lydia threatened to sue him if he tried to nullify their contract, he must have snapped."

"I think you should keep that theory to yourself."

"Listen to me. We both know he gave her those samples for publicity. Joey never hands out samples before a show. Why did he do it last night? He planned this. Think of the publicity he'll get now."

"Shhh!" Teresa jerked her thumb toward the curtain separating us. "There's a buyer in there. She might hear you."

I froze. If they pulled the curtain open, there'd be no way to pretend I hadn't heard. I stepped back but kept listening.

"The police were very interested in what I told them about Joey," Chryssinda said, this time in a barely audible whisper.

"You talked to the police? How could you? If they come after Joey, he'll lose everything."

"He should have thought of that before he tangled with Lydia."

17

BANG BANG

I took another step back and bumped into the table. The cup of espresso fell over and spilled onto my line sheets. I grabbed the mound of samples to get them out of the path of liquid and looked around for something to blot the spill.

It was a bad time for me to pop out from behind the private vendor appointment partition and announce my presence. It was a bad time for me to be anywhere at Intimate Mode, at least until I had a chance to find out who knew what and why, but one thing was certain: there was more to Lydia's death than met the eye. Considering the photo of her backside on the cover of the *Las Vegas Sun*, there was a whole lot of *her* that met the eye. I had two more days to work the trade show, and I had to use that time wisely.

Aside from the front entrance that would have put me in the path of Teresa and Chryssinda, there was one other way out. Under the pipe and drape that separated Cheeky Panties from the booth behind them.

I pulled my lanyard off and shoved it into my laptop bag. I mopped up the spilled espresso with a pair of pink cotton Cheeky panties and thrust the soiled sample into the bottom of my laptop bag too, and then ducked under the back curtain.

I'd successfully gotten away from Joey Cheeks' booth, but I hadn't given much thought to the location where I'd turn up. Face to face with a pair of ankles, one of which was tattooed with a small ink-black fleur-de-lis. I stood up.

"Oh my gosh, you scared me!" said the owner of the ankles, a curvaceous black woman in a plush white terrycloth robe. "You're the sub? I'm Lisa."

"I'm Samantha."

She glanced at my body. "I told them I needed somebody with some meat on their bones. Turn around."

I turned.

"Hard to tell when you got all your clothes on."

"One of the models called me fluffy," I offered.

She checked me out and nodded. "You'll do. Did they give you a sample when you got here?"

I shook my head.

She picked up a garment. "Here," she said. "You better hurry up and change because we're supposed to hit the floor in ten minutes and your makeup needs a boost."

"I'm not—I don't think—"

"Girl, is this your first intimate apparel show?

Please." She pulled her terrycloth robe open like a flasher and Bam! It was cleavage and hips. "This is about female empowerment. Women see us in this product, they see themselves in this product. Men see us in this product, they see confidence. Either way, we go out there like this, and buyers write orders. That's our job. You model sunglasses? You show them your face because that's where the sunglasses go. You model shoes? You show them your feet because that's where the shoes go."

I looked at the black garment. It must be some sort of sleepwear. "What are we modeling today?"

She turned around and handed me a tube of red lipstick. "What do you think? You gonna show them your bang bang, because that's where the lingerie goes."

My bang bang?

She grabbed my laptop bag. "Do you have any other shoes in your model bag?"

She flipped the bag open, and I grabbed it from her.

"No, just the ones I'm wearing."

She frowned. "What size are you? Nine? Ten? Eleven? I got big feet, so you probably can't borrow any of mine—"

"Seven."

"Girl, how do you expect to keep your balance on size seven feet?" She shook her head. "You need to up your game if you want to make a career of this. You're already on the short side. Lucky for you this is the year of body diversity."

"I'm five seven," I said. "Five ten in my heels. Six if they're platforms."

"Honey, I'm six feet two in my bare black feet."

She tossed my bag along the wall next to a row of zipped and unzipped duffel bags. "Good thing nobody's going to be looking at our feet today. Put on the sample and then come out front for your makeup. You don't have a lot of time to stand around and chat."

She left. I had one moment of indecision. Go back to Joey Cheeks' booth and explain I'd overheard rumors to the effect that their designer was an unstable murderer or put on a nightgown and prepare to show my bang bang with a group of models before coming back here and making a break for it.

It was a tough choice.

I stripped down to my pink strapless push-up bra and matching bikini panties and pulled the nightgown over my head. I left the privacy of the changing booth and joined the models out front.

Oh, no. These weren't just any nightgowns. They were Naughty Nighties. And every single one of the models was in the same black garment that I was. The same black garment that I hadn't bothered to look at in the mirror.

We were dressed like cops.

Well, the kind of cops who show up at bachelor parties and remove our uniforms to the beat of a boom box.

Oh, no!

Before I could run screaming back to Joey Cheeks, an Amazonian blonde grabbed my hair and twisted it up on top of my head. She pulled a police cap over it and then came at me with a makeup brush. "Girl, you need to watch some makeup tutorials. This foundation is busted," she said. "Can't work miracles. Good thing they won't be looking at your face."

Not looking at my feet. Not looking at my face. I wasn't enthused by the process of elimination.

She swatted at my cheekbones and nose with a fluffy brush. "Okay, you're ready for the raid."

"The raid?"

A police siren sounded. Lisa came up behind me and, with her hands on my waist, inched me forward like we were doing a conga line. "You know the drill, right? When the siren stops, you go."

"Go where?"

"Out there. Run to the stage. Make as much noise as you want. The whole point of this is to draw attention to us, and we draw attention to Yarvi."

"What's Yarvi?"

"Not what—who. She's the designer." Lisa looked at me funny. "Are you okay? Did you eat some of that bad sushi from the VIP room?"

"I was late checking in," I said. "I didn't get all the details."

"Here's the drill. The siren stops, we charge the runway. Once we've gotten everyone's attention, Yarvi comes out and shoots panties into the crowd. You'll know her when you see her. Tall redhead with a shoulder cannon."

"Once we turn everything over to her, we're done?"

"Pretty much," she said. "Just do what I do."

I formed a new plan. Charge the stage. Hide in the back. Disappear when everybody was paying attention to the tall redhead with the cannon. Get back to the booth, grab my laptop bag, and leave.

I could do this.

The police siren wiped out conversation. As we filtered out of the booth and into running-to-the-stage position, I realized what a perfect opportunity this was. None of the vendors would be paying attention to their booths, not while we were running, not while we were on stage, and not after Yarvi had taken the mic and hijacked everyone's attention. What I needed was to get back to the booth behind Joey's, get my things, and get the heck out of there while the getting was good.

The siren *Woop! Woop! Wooped!* for another solid minute. Just when the noise level was borderline unbearable, it stopped. The crowd cheered, and then I was carried in a swell of models clad in Naughty Nightie cop costumes toward the main stage.

Remember the plan, Samantha.

The runway was in the back corner of the convention center, so our journey carried us out of the Blue section, through Orange, Pink, and Green, and past Ingenue, the aisle of emerging designers (White). I temporarily lost myself in the cheerleading team sensation, clapping and laughing and enjoying the company of the other models. Lisa grabbed my hand and pulled me up the stairs.

"You're doing great!" she said. She turned her back toward the audience, bent over, and flashed her panties to the crowd.

"Thanks," I said. "This is fun!" I clapped my hands and hopped about a bit like the other models. From our position on the platform, I had a fantastic vantage point —or I would have if I could see over the heads of the other women. Under normal circumstances, my five-foot-seven height plus three- or four-inch heels would have helped me see over anyone in front of me, but this time I was the shortest of the bunch.

As the rest of them teased the audience with raunchy moves that seemed more appropriate for an after-hours venue, I peeked between elbows, waists, and in one case, thighs, scanning the room until I spotted an altercation at the fringes of the crowd.

Even from a distance, I recognized Joey Cheeks' Elvis style. He was arguing with Teresa at the back of the crowd, blocking my view of the vendors set up in the White aisle. Where I'd had the intellect to at least attempt to go undercover, he would easily be picked out of a lineup. Although, recalling the number of Elvis impersonators currently working in Vegas, perhaps he wouldn't.

I moved to the right, behind a row of models, trying to get a better view. Two of the women moved behind me, and as they danced, I got bumped to the front of the pack.

I tuned out the panty raid and focused all my attention on Joey and Teresa. He spoke something directly into her ear. Her face contorted with anger. He let go of her. She turned toward him and pushed his chest forcefully. Joey stepped back a few feet, and Teresa took off down the aisle.

Joey glanced at the stage and then followed Teresa. I shifted my weight from foot to foot in a poor display of dancing and watched them disappear around the corner.

If they were headed back to Joey's booth, they'd no doubt catch me when I returned for my things. Especially if the rest of the venue was standing in a pack around the stage in the corner. As I stood in front of massive numbers of people, I felt my whole plan dissolve before my eyes. I couldn't imagine how things could possibly get worse.

And then I felt hands grabbing at my costume. I looked at the other models, and seconds before reality hit, my Naughty Nightie cop costume was torn off in breakaway fashion, leaving me on the stage in my pink push-up bra and panties.

So much for undercover.

18

THE NEAREST INSANE ASYLUM

PLAN, SHMAN. I NEEDED OUT OF THERE, STAT!

Recap of problems: My clothes were in a booth in the middle of the convention center. At least one person who I suspected of being involved in a faked suicide/murder was within five feet of that booth. And I was on a stage in my underwear.

Amidst bouncing boobs and butts clad in colorful bra-and-panty sets, a tall redhead took the stage. Judging from the model and crowd reaction, that was Yarvi. She held what looked like a military assault rifle. She raised it in front of her and fired over the heads of the crowd.

The panty cannon. Yarvi was shooting panty samples at the audience, and the audience was going wild. Buyers who had earlier milled about acting as if a convention center of women in underwear was the most sophisticated venue in the world elbowed each other out of the way like desperate bachelorettes clamoring to catch the bouquet at a wedding.

Amidst the melee, I maneuvered my way to the back of the stage, and the hat fell off my head. In addition to my more pressing problems was the fact that I wasn't wearing Yarvi's underwear line. Any focus on my skivvies would detract from her brand message, not strengthen it. I could use that to my benefit. When I was all the way behind the rest of the women, I slipped off the stage and ducked underneath. Feet stomped over my head like a production of *A Chorus Line*. On hands and knees, I crawled from one side to the other and waited.

For what, I didn't know. What I did know was I needed a new plan.

After a painfully long time, the sound of feet on my ceiling scattered. The panty raid was over. If I'd spent more time studying my schedule, I would have known whether the stage was going to be used for another presentation, but I didn't. And every single piece of information or information-gathering methods I had were in my laptop bag in a row of models' gear in the booth behind Joey Cheeks' booth. My schedule. My lanyard. My phone.

My pride.

The only thing that was available was the black fabric that was attached to the stage to serve as the skirt to cover the platform.

I've worn crazier outfits.

But removing the skirt from the platform and

fashioning it into some sort of garment would draw unnecessary attention to me while I tried to make a getaway.

I briefly wondered, when Nick asked himself "What would Samantha do?" if he considered the possibilities of hiding under the stage of a major industry trade show in his underwear and the difficulties that lie in the near future. I certainly hoped not. Asking himself that question might lead him to reexamine his decision to invite me into his family.

If there were one place where I could walk around in my underwear and not attract attention, the lingerie show was it. If only I had a friend. If only I had someone inside the show, a designer friend who I could rely on for help. If only—

Amanda Ries.

I crawled to the end of the platform and peeked out between two panels of fabric. The audience had dissipated, but not entirely. Trousered legs stood nearby. Men's trousers, which meant buyers or vendors but not models. That was no good. I needed camouflage, and in this venue, that meant other women in their underwear like me. I readjusted myself to a more comfortable position and waited.

The opportunity presented itself when a group of naked legs appeared to my left. One set of the legs was chocolate brown and curvy and had a small fleur-de-lis tattooed on her ankle. With any luck, there was only one curvy black model with a fleur-de-lis tattooed on her ankle, and it was Lisa. And considering I was in Vegas, it seemed fitting to wish for luck.

When the legs were in front of me, I opened a small slit between panels of the black stage skirt. "Psssst! Lisa!"

Lisa stopped. She turned her feet away from me and then toward me. "Did somebody say something?"

"Psssst! Down here!" I pushed the black fabric so it fluttered out toward her legs and then fluttered back down into place.

The feet stepped away from me.

I lifted the fabric and peeked underneath. "I need a favor."

"Oh, girl, no."

"Get Amanda Ries. She's a designer in the White aisle. Tell her there's a woman under the stage who needs her help. She'll know it's me."

Lisa's feet turned and left. I curled up in a ball and hugged my knees. Had I done the right thing? There was a very good chance that letting Amanda decide what to do meant my next outfit would be a jacket that buckled in the back while men in white uniforms took me to the nearest insane asylum.

Or maybe in Amanda's world, what to do meant calling Nick. I'd never considered "What would Amanda do?" and a tiny part of me was really, really happy my life hadn't come to that. Except Amanda wasn't the one under the stage in her underwear, so maybe it had come to that. I didn't know what Amanda would do, but my only option at this point was to wait and find out.

A curious thing happens when you spend any amount of time in the dark. Like a sensory deprivation tank, my other senses tuned in to what my eyes couldn't see. Only a small sliver of light penetrated my surroundings from under the hem of the nylon stage skirt, and even that disappeared when there was no movement on the other side. When the skirt was still, I knew I was alone. When the skirt moved, I knew people were present.

The moving skirt comforted me more than the still one. The lack of movement anywhere but the hem of the stage skirt comforted me in a no-critters-here way. The sliver of light comforted me more than the movement of the fabric. So when the sliver of light vanished and left me in total darkness under the stage, I almost screamed.

There's a reason people are afraid of the dark. It's because the dark is freaking scary!

The black fabric buckled inward. It hit my arm, and I flinched. The toe of a loafer appeared under the hem of the skirt. I recognized the loafer because I had the very same pair in my closet. It was one of Nick's designs. And I knew of at least one person at the trade show who had a more than fifty percent chance of wearing one of Nick's designs other than me.

My suspicions were confirmed when the loafer kicked a pink silk robe under the stage. Even if I could see the tag, I wouldn't have wasted time trying to read it. I found the sleeves and pulled the robe on, held the front shut with one hand, and pushed the stage fabric aside. There were too many people around. If I crawled out from under the stage, someone would see me.

I bunched the robe up to my waist and used the belt to bind the excess fabric to my torso, and then I crawled. Away from the loafers. Away from the White aisle. Away from the front of the stage. I thought. But when I got to the very back, I peeked under the hem and realized I miscalculated where I'd end up.

I'd expected the coast to be clear, but it wasn't. A woman stood alone with a phone to her ear. I recognized the track pants and satin bomber jacket immediately: Teresa Kander. I dropped the black fabric and closed my eyes, listening to her conversation.

"I did everything you asked," Teresa said. "Everything. Lydia's out of the picture just like you wanted." She paused for a beat. "I don't care how it looks for you. I want my money, and I want out."

19

CRAY CRAY

THOSE WERE INCRIMINATING WORDS. OR NOT. OUT OF context, everybody sounded guilty. I wanted to crawl out from under the platform, chase Teresa, and demand to know who was on the other end of that call. I listened for more of the conversation, but all I heard was silence. When I peeked past the black nylon fabric, Teresa was gone.

And then, while I was looking around for something to verify that I hadn't imagined the eavesdropped-on conversation with Teresa, the recognizable designer loafers reentered my view.

"We need to talk," Amanda said.

"You took the words right out of my mouth."

IN A WAY, I was lucky. Nobody in the intimate apparel industry knew me except those I'd met at my appointment at Joey Cheeks this morning, so as long as Amanda and I gave the Blue section of the convention center a wide berth, the odds of me being labeled an imposter were low. Two very specific things helped improve those odds: me being in a robe and underwear, and Amanda being one of the participating designers. As long as I stayed with her, we appeared to be a designer instructing one of her hired models. Thanks to the new movement toward body inclusivity, my sandwich and pretzel curves weren't the red flag they might have been just five years ago.

Avoiding Joey's aisle meant not getting my personal items. Amanda and I left the convention center and went to the one place Joey Cheeks wouldn't turn up: the casino ladies' room.

It was slightly over the top. Mauve marble fixtures and floors, white porcelain sinks filled with river rocks and a cascade of water that could have solved California's ongoing drought problem lined the far wall. A tufted pink velvet sofa sat under a six-foot-wide mirror that was mounted in an elaborate gold frame. Wall sconces glowed with soft pink lights that gave our complexions a pretty glow. Note to self: replace all light bulbs with pink ones. Better than a hundred-dollar moisturizer.

I checked under the bathroom stalls (you can't be too careful) and then joined Amanda on the sofa.

"Are you going to tell Nick?" I asked. I braced myself

for "yes" or "maybe" or "probably" or "what's it worth to keep me quiet?"

"No," she said.

"Why not?"

"Because he's my friend and you make him happy."

"But—"

She held her hand palm-side out.

The first time I'd met Amanda, we'd been passive forces in opposition. I'd since learned that she was a case of what you see is what you get. Amanda didn't have an inner amateur sleuth like I did. She didn't need to seek justice or uncover the truth. (She probably didn't like standardized tests either.) She wanted her life to be uncomplicated, and when it had been complicated, she'd just about melted down.

I'd been the one to solve her problems, and while that hadn't awarded me a friendship ring, it had leveled the playing field. And now that I knew a little bit about her college roommate's suicide and the roommate's relationship with Nick, I understood it was tragedy that bound them, not a past romance. Judging from the guilty feelings Nick carried with him, I doubted he'd ever viewed Amanda as a potential girlfriend. It was a question I'd wondered about for a long time, and I'd now reached a reasonable conclusion.

"I have about ten minutes until my next appointment," Amanda said, "and I'd rather you're not at the booth when he shows up, so this is going to be brief. Why were you under the stage in your underwear?"

"It was preferable to being *on* the stage in my underwear."

She didn't say anything for a few seconds. I braced myself for criticism of my insanity or vows to break me up from Nick to protect him.

"Did you see anything suspicious?"

"What?" I thought I heard her, but the question was so unexpected that I preferred to be sure before making a fool of myself with an answer.

"You probably had a good view of the audience while you were up on the stage. I'm guessing that's why you did it, right? Because what you did was either crazy or brave, and I think it's best for all of us if we go with brave."

Sure, except there wasn't anything brave about my actions. I'd ended up on that stage, not because I'd seen an opportunity to surveil the crowd, but because I'd needed an escape from Joey Cheeks' booth, and ducking out the back and joining Yarvi's girl squad was my chicken way of hiding. It was typical Samantha luck that my escape plan had backfired on me. And while I could have kept all that to myself, if Amanda and I were ever going to have a relationship that wasn't rooted in contention, this was my opportunity to take a step in that direction.

"Do you really believe I would strip down to my underwear in a public venue to get a better view of someone who might have something to hide?"

"Isn't that what you did?"

"Well, yes, but it wasn't as well-thought-out as all that."

There are times in one's life when one knows what one should do. The right thing. And I recognized this was one of those times. I had to do something I never expected to do: confide in Amanda. If she was willing to keep this whole escapade a secret from Nick simply because she knew I made him happy, then I had to accept that her friendship with him made him happy. And if that meant—

Oh, f**k it.

"I was in Joey Cheeks' booth when his line manager, Teresa, came in with the newspaper that announced Lydia's death. He said some pretty crude things about her that make me wonder if maybe we shouldn't look a little more closely at their relationship. And then I heard Chryssinda tell Teresa that he might have killed her to break her contract. I had to get out of there, but the only way out was under the pipe and drape behind his booth. I ended up in Yarvi's booth, where I was mistaken for a substitute model. I didn't have any idea what was happening until I was on that stage and the models tore off my uniform."

Amanda's face went through an assortment of expressions while I talked: disbelief, surprise, and, finally, shock. And then she giggled.

Her giggle was contagious. I giggled too, and then, like a release valve, the giggles turned into full-on laughter that bordered on hysteria. I hadn't realized how much anxiety I'd built up over the course of the day until now, and I had Amanda Ries to thank.

Las Vegas deserved every ounce of reputation it had. People got cray-cray out here.

Amanda checked her watch. "I need to get back to the booth." She stood up. "What about you?"

I looked down at my robe, considered my options, and looked up. "Do you mind if I borrow this for the rest of the day?"

20

MAC AND CHEESE

Amanda and I went separate directions. She returned to the White aisle, and I stopped into the Flush newsstand and scanned the articles about Lydia. I would have bought copies, but with my wallet still in Yarvi's booth, I was broke.

Which I realized again when I tried to take the Deuce. The driver raised his eyebrows at my attire and turned me away.

By the time I arrived at The Left Bank, it was after six. I was hot, my feet were swollen, and I wanted comfort food. Sadly, for everything Las Vegas boasted in their advertising campaigns, they lacked pretzels, my snack food of choice.

I stumbled to the front desk. "Meees Keeed," Jacque said. "How can I help you today?" His eyes shifted back and forth between my face and my (Amanda's) robe.

"I lost my keycard," I said.

"Your room on ze sixth floor?"

"No, I'm in the Napoleon Room."

He looked confused.

"It's a long story."

He tapped the keyboard a few times. "My system shows you checked out this morning," he said. "You do not have a current reservation."

"Oh yes, I do. I don't check out for another three days." Do not panic. "Can you look up Nick Taylor?"

"*Non*, there is no Nick Taylor in our system either." He smiled. "Would you like me to see what we have available?"

"What about Marc Rico?"

"I cannot give out personal information about our guests, Meees Keeed," he said.

I'd had just about enough of secrets and lies and people pretending to be something they weren't. I wanted to relax. And to sample at least half of the twenty-two versions of mac and cheese from the room service menu. And to change into real clothes, not a (very soft!) robe from Amanda's collection.

I leaned forward until I was as close to Jacques as the marble counter would allow. "I know that you know that I know Marc Rico and Nick Taylor, and if you don't tell me where they are in the next five minutes, I'm going to create a scene right here in the lobby."

His eyes widened, and his voice dropped to a whisper. "Allow me to ring Mr. Reeeco."

I stood upright and attempted a smile. I'd left this

morning with my doubts about Marc's past and present, but it appeared as though he held the key to my immediate future.

"Mr. Reeeco, I have a Samantha Keeed here at ze front desk. She asked me to ring your room—*oui*. I see. Of course. I will tell her. Thank you, Mr. Reeeco."

Jacques hung up. "Meees Keeed—"

I glared at him.

"Mr. Reeeco made arrangements to move your bill under his account." He picked up a keycard and recoded it. "As a guest of Mr. Reeeco, you are entitled to complimentary use of our amenities, including ze Left Bank Spa." He glanced at my robe again. "If there eees anything else you need, please let me know. I am sorry for ze inconvenience."

Why the sudden attitude change? Jacques already knew I knew Marc from the very first time I tried to check in. Pretending to be surprised by Marc's generosity was suspicious. If just knowing Marc was the reason for Jacques' attitude change, I should have been getting this treatment all along.

I took the keycard and left. There was something fake about Jacques, and it wasn't just his accent.

———

THE NAPOLEON ROOM WAS UNOCCUPIED. I set the new keycard on my end table and went directly to the bathroom for a shower. Once clean, I dressed in my black capri pants, a loose black tunic with a halter neckline, and a pale-pink brooch shaped like the sun in the center of the neckline. I styled my hair, did a full face of makeup, and added earrings and bracelets.

In the time it took me to do all that, Nick didn't return. After another ten minutes of wiping off the red lipstick left over from my stint on stage and replacing it with a more subdued mauve shade that matched the brooch, I called down to the front desk.

"Mr. Rico, how can I help you?" answered a female voice.

"This isn't Mr. Rico. It's Miss Kidd. Samantha Kidd."

"Ah. Mr. Rico's guest. How may I help you?"

"Why did you think I was Mr. Rico?"

"Your room number flashed up on the screen, and the screen indicates that the room is booked to Mr. Rico."

"You know all that from one phone call?"

"It is our job to take care of our best clients," she said. "Mr. Rico is very special to us, and we want to keep him happy. As his guests, that applies to you as well. Is there something special you would like me to arrange? Dinner reservations? A show?"

"Do you have access to today's newspaper?"

"Of course. I'll have the *Las Vegas Sun* sent right up."

"Yes, and, um, do you have any others? The less legitimate ones?"

She paused. "I'll have an assortment of Las Vegas daily newspapers sent to your room."

I thanked her and hung up. My next call was to room

service. A little mac and cheese wouldn't spoil my appetite should Nick want dinner.

It wasn't long after the papers arrived that I confirmed my earlier suspicion. The same photo that I'd seen in the trashy newspaper at Intimate Mode appeared in every paper that ran the notice of Lydia's death. I called the *Las Vegas Sun,* the most reputable of the bunch.

"Hi. I'm calling about the photo of the lingerie model you ran in today's paper. I noticed the same photo appeared in other publications. Do you have contact information?"

"Hold, please," said a bored voice. Jazzy music filled the headset. While I waited, I spread the various newspapers out on the bed.

When the story on me from the *Ribbon Eagle/Times* was picked up by the AP wire, there had been one accompanying photo. The original "Local Girl Does Good" puff piece had been pitched with the terms that the photo shoot be a staged day of me at work, styling a page for Tradava's upcoming catalog. The intent was that the merchandise—and the store—would get double exposure.

As it turned out, the pictures from the shoot were confiscated as evidence in an investigation. The lone photo that appeared with the article had been taken by the delivery van driver from Tradava. He'd wanted something to show his family. The reprint rights had paid him more than his Tradava severance package, and an unflattering view of me goofing around in front of a rack of samples had landed in over a hundred newspapers across the country.

I learned two things from that experience: when newspapers want a photo to accompany a news piece, they have standard payment terms for acquisition. And to collect on those payment terms, the photographer had to sign a release. So even if the photo credit was withheld upon request in print, the newspaper would have documentation to prove they'd fulfilled their end of the bargain.

"Hello?" said the bored voice.

"I'm here," I said.

"Yeah, you wanted to know about the photo of Lydia Moss?"

"Yes, please."

"The paper acquired full rights. It's ours now. You want to reprint it like everybody else?"

"No, I'm looking for the photographer."

"'Alain Remie' is the name on the contract. I can't give out more than that."

I was stunned. "That's all I need. Thank you."

As I hung up, I couldn't help but consider the third thing I'd learned from my experience at Tradava: when a camera is aimed at you, smile. It was a good thing no cameras were aimed in my direction because this information was anything but cheerful.

Alain Remie was the hotel manager who had shown up with the police the day I'd reported Lydia's body.

21

MAXIMUM SLEUTHING TIME

I DROPPED ONTO THE BED TO CONSIDER WHAT THIS MEANT. Alain Remie had arrived at Nick's and my room after we called the police. It might be standard procedure for the hotel management to be notified, especially here. If one phone call to the front desk could elicit the hotel service I'd experienced an hour ago, then sure. And I'd seen *Ocean's Eleven*. There was always someone watching in a Las Vegas hotel.

Alain Remie had known about Lydia's body lying outside on the sidewalk before the police had arrived. He'd taken photos and financially benefitted from them. Surely there was a conflict of interest in there somewhere? If it got out that the manager of a hotel of this magnitude was selling photos of guests, The Left Bank would be ruined.

I closed my eyes and thought back to the image of

Lydia's body. I'd known almost immediately that it was her from her hair, her T-shirt, and her wedding veil. But the photo in the papers had been taken from a different angle, one that caught the #GetCheeky slogan on her panties. It was as if the photographer—Mr. Remie, I now knew—had it in mind to include it in the frame. And as I considered who would benefit from such a photo, one clear person came to mind: Joey Cheeks. Right now, he was the person with the most to gain from Lydia's death to the tune of free publicity across the news. But that meant the position of her body hadn't been accidental— which was a whole other level of creepy.

More and more, Lydia's death was looking relevant to her line of work. Good thing I had two more days to work the Intimate Mode show for Tradava. Tomorrow, I'd rearrange my schedule for maximum sleuthing time.

———

I WAS BETWEEN my second and third room service orders of mac and cheese (lobster vs. truffle) when the keycard clicked in the door. I jumped to my feet and raced to open it, eager to share with Nick everything I'd found out. But Nick's greeting was halted by his appearance—shirt open at the collar, necktie loosened, jacket in hand—and scent, which was decidedly not the Creed Bois du Portugal cologne I bought him for his recent birthday. It was more like Eau du Public Transportation.

"I'm sorry," he said.

"For what?" I shut the door behind him. "I'm the one who should apologize. I didn't know how long you would be, so I ordered room service."

"You don't need to apologize for ordering room service. Trust me when I say I need to apologize and you don't."

"Why? We're both here to work. I figured your day went longer than you expected. Trade shows can be overwhelming, and sometimes you have to do things you didn't think you'd have to do to get the job done." I weighed the pros and cons of admitting I'd revealed my bang bang on stage. Maybe there was a different way to describe my day.

Nick put his hands on my shoulders, his arms straight out in front of him. "I need to take a shower, and then we need to talk. Because I'm having serious second thoughts about, well, about everything. What happened today was a little more than I signed up for, and I don't know if I can do this."

I felt like I'd been punched in the gut. Amanda must have told him. She lied about keeping my participation in the panty raid a secret, and now I was going to have to explain to Nick that I'd been mostly naked in a public venue today. Worse, it had been fun. How to explain that?

Nick had accepted an awful lot of unusual behavior from me in the past, but this must have crossed a line. The biggest gamble of my life was betting on a future with him, and our engagement was about to crap out over my perfectly innocent participation in a lingerie exhibition.

"Hey," he said. "Why are you crying?"

"I'm a good gamble," I said. I tried to blink back the second wave of tears that formed, but they spilled onto my recently applied makeup and cut tracks down my cheeks.

"Kidd, I never said you weren't. You're the most full-of-life person I've ever met. That's why I keep thinking about what you would think, or what you would like or what you would do. Your brain works in unexpected ways, and I love that about you."

"So why do you want to break off our engagement?"

Surprise and confusion clouded Nick's face. "I don't. But when I tell you why I was late coming back, you might."

I cradled his face in my hands. "No matter what you did today, I probably did worse." I thought about the three orders of mac and cheese I'd eaten on my own. "Way worse."

"Not possible."

Inhale. Exhale. Look Nick straight in his root-beer-barrel-colored eyes. "Earlier today, I had a Naughty Nightie cop costume torn off to reveal my underwear. While I was on stage. In front of the attendees of Intimate Mode. And then I hid under the stage for hours until Amanda found me. I'm pretty sure whatever you did can't beat that."

Nick cleared his throat. I braced myself for "when will

you learn?" or "you are insane," or "you were right, I can't do this."

"Kidd, for the past four hours I've been in a holding cell at the Las Vegas police station on suspicion of solicitation."

22

QUESTIONS

I was keeping the mac and cheese secret to myself.

"Is this one of those things I need to accept and not ask questions?" I asked.

"If it were me, I'd have questions."

"I know. I'm usually on the receiving end of conversations like this. I've heard the questions."

"I'll explain everything, but before I do, I'd like two things."

"What?"

"A shower and some of that mac and cheese I smell."

At least we were still in sync on priorities.

We were on our third day in Las Vegas, and already I'd learned it was a town of excess. The lesson took hold when the fourth room service order showed up. "Thanks,

Fred," I said. I tipped my head toward Nick and signed the check unapologetically. There were worse sins in Vegas than overindulging in expensive mac and cheese.

Nick, fresh from his shower, joined me on the sofa. He'd changed into a black polo shirt and jeans. I wheeled the room service cart into the room and transferred our plates to the coffee table in front of us.

"Aren't you going to eat?" Nick asked. I detected a note of worry in his voice.

"Of course I'm going to eat." I picked up my fork and took a bite.

Nick seemed to relax and took a bite too.

I set my fork down. "Solicitation? For real? What were you thinking? Oh my God, I know what you were thinking. You did it again, didn't you?"

Nick set his fork down. "What do you think I was thinking?"

"You were thinking 'What would Samantha do?' Am I right?" I could tell from the look on his face I was right. "Stop it! Stop asking yourself that. It only gets you into trouble."

"I'm starting to see that."

———

MAC AND CHEESE turned into foreplay, which turned into both of us losing our clothes. The sun went down, and the twinkling lights from the Las Vegas Strip provided unique ambient lighting through the long, sheer curtains that maintained our privacy. As I lay next to him in the dark, thinking about everything that had happened since we'd arrived, there was one question that rose above the others. On top of who killed Lydia, where the pages from the wedding chapel guestbook were, what Joey Cheeks and Teresa Kander were arguing about, and how the hotel manager got away with selling an unauthorized photo of Lydia's body the day she died, there was one question that trumped them all. But Nick's soft snoring was sign enough that my question would wait until tomorrow.

When the bright sunlight flooded the room the next morning, I was no closer to figuring out the answer.

So I propped myself up on my elbow and prodded Nick awake. "Hey, Nick? Why did you think I'd solicit a prostitute?"

23

QUESTIONED

The answer turned out to be remarkably simple.

"Remember when Marc told us how he met Lydia?" Nick asked. "He used an escort service that catered to rich men. We know Lydia was the escort. I thought about you and how you always focus on the victim, so I thought what do we know about Lydia?"

So far, so good. So far, no prostitutes.

"We know Lydia was engaged to Marc. They met through a high-class escort service. She was a lingerie model." He ticked the items off on his fingers. "I figured Marc would answer my questions about their engagement, and you had the lingerie model aspect covered with Intimate Mode, so it was up to me to explore the other thing."

"You frequented a brothel?"

"Not exactly. I asked around to find out how one

might contact a high-class escort service. I asked one person too many, and that person turned me in for suspicion of solicitation."

"Were you arrested?"

"No, I was questioned."

"By Detective Marbury? It would be great if it was him. He'd understand why you wanted to know."

"No. Besides, does Detective Loncar usually understand when you start asking questions about his investigations?"

Good point.

Nick was referring to my somewhat contentious relationship with the homicide detective back home in Ribbon. It had taken a couple of years and more than one investigation for us to reach a level of mutual respect (my words).

I called down to room service for a hotel breakfast of waffles and ice cream. It wasn't listed on the regular room service menu, but me and room service were tight by now, and I took a chance they'd be open to the request. They were. By the time the food arrived, I had a new suggestion.

"I could call Loncar," I said. "Cops talk to other cops, right? I could call Detective Loncar and ask him to call Detective Marbury and tell him we're on the level."

"Don't do that."

"Why? That's what I would do."

"I know," Nick said. "That's what I'm afraid of."

"Okay, for now, I'll think like you and not call Detective Loncar." I sat on the bed and spooned soft vanilla ice cream onto my waffles. "You never told me what happened when you went to the police station."

"I didn't talk to Marbury," Nick said. "I talked to an officer from Vice. I told him about Marc's engagement, how he met his fiancée, and how, to protect him, I wanted to find out if the escort service was going to target him while he was in mourning."

I was impressed. "Way to use the facts to make your lie sound more believable, Taylor." I slugged his bicep.

He caught my fist and held it in the palm of his hand. "It wasn't a lie. Everything I said was the truth. And they already knew all of it anyway. Marc told them about the escort service when he talked to the police."

"He did?"

Nick nodded. "The more I think about this whole thing, the more I wonder about Marc getting hitched in the first place. The man is forty. He's been a lifelong bachelor. He employed a service to get him dates. The signs don't exactly point to the altar."

"But he was happy. You saw him, right?"

"He said he was happy. And within the hour, we were on our way to being kicked out of a casino bar for public drunkenness. The night before he was supposed to tie the knot. Again, sounds like something was off."

"Yes, and that something agrees with what Chaplain Rick told us. That the marriage was troubled from the start," I said.

"Yeah, there's that." Nick picked up a waffle and took a bite.

I stared at him.

"What?" he asked. "It's you and me in a hotel room in Vegas. I didn't think you'd judge me if I ate with my hands."

Emotions bubbled up within me. "I ate four orders of mac and cheese last night," I said. I didn't look away.

He set the waffle down. I waited for his response. He swallowed and said, "I love you, Kidd."

We finished our breakfast and got ready. Where other couples might say, "Have a nice day, honey!" before going separate directions, we mixed things up.

"Hey Kidd, try to keep your clothes on," Nick said.

"Will do. Try not to hire any hookers."

———

As previously arranged, I met Amanda in the lobby outside the lingerie show. She wore a white blazer, white T-shirt, and white trousers with silver loafers. I wore her pink satin robe over my black sheath dress. It was an hour before Intimate Mode opened to the attendees, but vendors were allowed entrance to prepare their booths for the day. Amanda signed me in as one of her models, and I followed her far enough to keep up appearances. When we reached the White aisle, I took off the robe.

"I'm going to get my things from Yarvi's booth while the coast is clear."

Amanda took the robe, and we split up. I made sure to go down the back aisle to the booth behind Joey's so as not to be spotted. My clothes were where I'd left them, balled up and discarded against the wall where the model duffel bags had lain. I grabbed my overstuffed bag and peeked out front. The lights had not been turned on, and the interior felt deserted.

I could get back to Amanda's booth, stash my stuff, and go about my day.

Or I could sneak into Joey's booth and snoop.

I couldn't shake the idea that it would be easy for Nick and Amanda to see Marc as guilty. They both wanted someone to blame for Pamela Martin's actions in college, and Marc made an easy target. But I wasn't convinced that Marc was anything other than a man caught in the crosshairs of something unrelated to him. Something that I was in a position to discover.

Yesterday, I would have known what Nick would do: return to Amanda's booth and go about my day. But Nick was thinking like me, and that was an odd endorsement of my sleuthing abilities. Did it mean my instincts, though not well thought out, were right?

It was a good thing Nick wasn't here to monitor my decision-making.

I extended the strap on my bulging laptop bag and hung it across my chest, went to the back of Yarvi's booth, and lifted the fabric that separated her booth from Joey's. The trade show venue would open soon, and while it was risky to even try to snoop, this was my only chance.

But as I ducked under the fabric, I knew my instincts were wrong. Because instead of finding an opportunity to snoop, I found Chryssinda slumped in a folding chair.

24

SNAP OUT OF IT!

I FORGOT ABOUT NOT DRAWING ATTENTION TO MYSELF AND ran to Chryssinda's unconscious body. Her head hung at an awkward angle, and her arms were limp by her sides. Her long blond hair was pulled into a tight ponytail on top of her head and fell in a straight line behind her. She was dressed in a black bra and matching boy short panties. Her exposed body revealed very little body fat.

I checked for her pulse by her throat. It was faint, but it was present.

"Help!" I yelled. "This woman needs help. Help! Somebody!" There was no answer. I poked my head out of the front of Joey's booth. "Amanda!" I hollered at the top of my lungs. If Marlon Brando had yelled "Stella" at the very same time, I would have drowned him out. "Amanda!" I yelled again.

The raven-haired designer entered the Get Cheeky

booth with an expression that said she was horrified by my behavior. As soon as she saw Chryssinda, she froze.

"Get help. Get security. Get anybody. Hurry!"

Her eyes were glued to Chryssinda's body.

"Amanda, snap out of it! Either get help or stay here and I'll get help. Chryssinda is still alive, but I don't know for how long. She needs medical attention."

Amanda's eyes fluttered, and she swayed. I grabbed an abandoned white cup that sat on the floor next to Chryssinda, yanked the plastic lid off, and threw the contents at Amanda. The scent of cola filled the air. Watered-down brown liquid discolored her white outfit. She blinked a few times while soda dripped off her chin, and then she turned and ran.

I bent down next to Chryssinda. "Can you hear me?" I asked.

She did not respond.

"Do you know who did this to you?"

She did not respond.

"Please hold on until the paramedics reach you," I whispered urgently.

She did not respond.

Security officers arrived a few moments later. Amanda and I were ushered out of the way while medical staff attended to the model. There would be no way for me to give a statement without revealing I had entered Joey's booth an hour before the trade show opened to buyers.

I wondered, briefly, if Chryssinda had a reason to be there herself?

Right before I fled Joey's booth yesterday, I'd overheard Chryssinda tell Teresa her suspicions about Joey's behavior. I'd watched Joey and Teresa fight from my position on the stage right before my bang-bang moment. While I was hiding under the stage after baring 98% of me to the audience in a disrobing worthy of a professional stripper, I heard Teresa tell someone she had done what was expected and she wanted her money.

If Joey wasn't up to something, maybe Teresa was. It seemed likely that there was something up with Joey Cheeks & Company. One of his models was dead, and another was on her way. I didn't know what it meant, but it did seem as though the events were connected.

Detective Marbury, not surprisingly, arrived at Intimate Mode shortly thereafter. It seemed he agreed with me.

"Ms. Kidd," he said. "I understand you discovered Ms. Sykes?"

"Who?"

"Chryssinda Sykes, the woman on her way to the hospital. Did my men get her identity wrong?"

"No, they got it right. I found her. I didn't know her last name."

"But you do know her?"

"I met her. She was a model here at the show, and she's a friend of Marc Rico."

"The same Marc Rico who was engaged to the

lingerie model you discovered outside of your hotel window?"

"Yes. Except no. I mean, I don't know how to answer the question."

"These questions are pretty straightforward."

"I know. It's what I know—or don't know—that's all jumbled up."

The detective tipped his head and scratched at the bristles of his beard. "Ms. Kidd, you should know I checked you out. Standard procedure. I found out you have a colorful past."

"I don't think it's my past that's colorful. I just happen to get involved with colorful people."

"Murderers. Arsonists. Mafia."

"Like I said, colorful." I smiled, shooting for something like *Aren't I charming?*

"I talked to a Detective Loncar. Do you want to know what he told me?"

Detective Loncar would not describe my sleuthing efforts as charming.

"He said I should take you seriously. He said ignoring you or discounting what you say will only cost me valuable time in my investigation."

"He said that? Did he call me charming?"

"No." Marbury paused. "He also told me you were engaged, and your fiancé was a calming presence on you."

"Aw, that's sweet."

"Is this the same fiancé who was brought in yesterday for solicitation?"

This guy was tough. "He wasn't trying to pick up a hooker!" I said.

Several officers looked my way.

"Is there someplace else we can talk?"

If Detective Marbury were of the female persuasion, I would have led him to the ladies' room where Amanda and I had bonded yesterday. This being his town, he had something else in mind. We sat in the VIP lounge on the second floor of the convention center. Until the police permitted the venue to open, the only people inside would be other early birds like me.

Detective Marbury had the benefit of checking me out first. I was trusting him blindly. Every movie I'd ever seen that prominently featured Las Vegas told me the cops were on the take. And then, in a flash, I thought, "What would Nick do?"

Nick would cooperate with law enforcement.

And so I did.

"My first thought was that Lydia killed herself, but according to Marc, he and Lydia snuck off to get married that night. Why would she kill herself after that?" I tried to justify the order of events. They didn't fit. "If I were investigating anything, I'd definitely talk to Chaplain Rick at The Left Bank. He would have been one of the last people to see Lydia alive."

The detective made a note.

"And do you know Joey Cheeks?"

"Ms. Moss's employer, right?"

"Right. His booth is the one where I found Chryssinda's body. He's a lingerie designer, and Lydia was under contract as the face of his company. He wanted to fire her, and she threatened to sue him—at least that's what I overheard Chryssinda tell his line manager, Teresa Kander. Joey and Lydia didn't have a good relationship, and I'm not so sure he and Chryssinda did, either." I paused. "Plus I saw him argue with Teresa."

Marbury's brow furrowed. "Cheeks. Like Cheeky?"

"Yes. The panties Lydia had on the morning she died were from his collection. And that photo—the one that made it into the papers—"

"We're already on that."

"You know about Alain Remie?"

Marbury cocked his head. "Where did you get that name?"

"He's the hotel manager of The Left Bank. He came to our room the morning I called you, remember? He's the one who sold the picture to the *Las Vegas Sun*."

"How do you know that?"

"I called the paper and asked about the permission of rights form."

He stared at me. "You called the paper and asked about the permission of rights form," he repeated.

I nodded.

"Tell me about the solicitation charge," he said.

"The *suspicion of* solicitation charge," I corrected.

"Nick didn't solicit anything from anybody. He was just asking questions."

"Do you know why?"

"Yes, I know why, and you probably know why too."

"I'd like to hear it in your words."

"Nick wanted to make sure the escort service Marc used wasn't going to take advantage of him, so Nick poked around and asked questions about how one might find an escort service that specializes in that sort of clientele."

Marbury set his notepad and pen down and crossed his arms over his chest. "You bought that story?"

Okay, that just made me mad. "Nick did what he did because he asked himself what I would have done, and that's the single most romantic thing any man has ever done for me in my entire life. I'm not going to let a solicitation charge ruin it."

I told Detective Marbury what else I knew. When we finished, I felt an odd sense of relief, like the act of unburdening myself of the knowledge of suspicious ongoings of the people around me had left me lighter. Perhaps this was why people cooperated with the police. You tell them what you know, and you're done. You bear no further responsibility in what happens or whether the guilty party is caught. From here on out, it was someone else's craps game.

It must be the Vegas setting that made me add the word "craps" to my thoughts, right? Because I did what I was supposed to do. What Nick would have done. The police had the information needed to conduct their investigation. I was in an unfamiliar city, with no real resources, and a job that Tradava, my employer, expected me to do. Which was what I should have been focused on all along.

———

IN THE TIME I spent talking to Detective Marbury, Chryssinda had been moved from the Get Cheeky booth and sent to the hospital. The venue had argued with the police about the cost of hosting a trade show of this magnitude, the potential loss of future business, and the impact of shutting down for the rest of the day, and since nothing suspicious had been found (other than an unconscious model in one of the booths, which, apparently, wasn't all that unusual), the police allowed Intimate Mode to reopen. I suspected that had been their intent all along, but in putting up a fight, they made their point. Even in Las Vegas, the cost of doing business did not trump police procedure. A point made more evident when I saw Joey Cheeks leave the venue with Detective Marbury.

Now that I had my belongings, I checked in at registration and consulted my schedule. Tradava had left things light today: a trend presentation on the same stage I'd hidden under yesterday, a meet and greet with two 3-pack cotton panty vendors we already relied on for replenishment, and a cocktail reception for VIP clients. It was about time I forgot Marc Rico, Lydia Moss, Joey Cheeks, Chryssinda Sykes, Yarvi Tatum, Teresa Kander, Alain Remie, and anybody else who'd elbowed their way into my life since arriving in Vegas. I'd even give Amanda's booth a wide berth if possible.

I SPENT THE *balance of the day doing the job I was in Vegas to* do. When the lights flashed at six to indicate closing time, my laptop bag bulged with line sheets, vendor contacts, swag, and fabric swatches. I'd even had to drop yesterday's outfit at Will Call, the venue's package holding station, which was how I found myself in line with my claim check while others exited the show. I handed my ticket to the man behind the booth. When he returned, it was my bag of clothes, along with a small gift bag that said #GetCheeky.

"That's not mine," I said.

"Are you sure?" he asked.

He turned the bag around. On the outside, stapled on, was a business card for Teresa Kander with the #GetCheeky logo underneath. Written on the white card in pink marker was Samantha Kidd/ Tradava.

"Did you have an appointment with Joey Cheeks?" he asked.

"Yesterday," I said.

"They've been giving samples to their appointments. Did you get a swag bag?"

"No." I left out the fact that they hadn't exactly seen me leave, along with the fact that I wasn't particularly enthused to own a pair of #GetCheeky panties (unless they were Thursday).

"Teresa must have realized the oversight after you left and wanted to make sure you didn't feel slighted. She's very efficient." He glanced at my lanyard. "Especially if Tradava is a good account for them."

The jury was still out on that.

I thanked him and left. It wasn't until I was back in my room with my shoes off, hair up, and room service on the way (#17: mac and gruyere), that I went through my various vendor gifts. Thanks to the memory of the words on Lydia's underwear, I put off opening the #GetCheeky bag until last, which was why it took me forty-seven minutes after returning to The Left Bank to discover the connection I'd missed all along.

25

STANDARD TRADE SHOW
BEHAVIOR

Inside the #GetCheeky bag was a black cone bra reminiscent of Madonna's Blonde Ambition tour in 1991. Being a fan of Madonna, I recognized it immediately. I also remembered the last time I'd seen it. The day Nick and I arrived on the strip of Las Vegas when we'd watched an Elvis impersonator pose with a Madonna impersonator in front of the fake Eiffel Tower across the street.

My body buzzed with energized nerve endings. I dropped the cone bra and flipped through my belongings for my cell phone. I swiped through the recent photos until I found the one of Elvis and Madonna. I zoomed in and studied the fuzzy, blown-up image. I wasn't 100% sure about their identities, but I was over 95%. It was Joey Cheeks and Chryssinda Sykes. On the sidewalk where Lydia's body had been found less than twenty-four hours later.

Using my fingers, I moved the image around the screen. Elvis held a selfie-stick aimed at the two of them. The angle was an unflattering one: camera held low and aimed up. Knowing what I did from my own attempts to get flattering selfies, the camera should be slightly above the subject's head. That would reduce the appearance of chins, make the head appear larger than the hips, create a shadow by the décolletage, and allow the natural sunlight to reflect off foreheads and cheeks and create the appearance of a glow from within.

Chryssinda, being a model, would have known all of that. So why would she allow Joey to capture such an unflattering angle?

Maybe Joey hadn't been taking their picture. Maybe he had pretended to clown around while really he was interested in what was behind them. The very location where Lydia's body was found. Could I be looking at Joey Cheeks casing a possible murder site?

Joey had a motive. Lydia was under contract to him, and he made no secret of the fact that he wanted her out. But why was Chryssinda unconscious in his booth? Had she figured something out too and confronted him? Had he been in the process of shutting her up permanently when he was interrupted, thus leaving her still alive?

I set my phone down and picked up the Madonna bra. If I was right, and Chryssinda had been wearing this, then someone wanted me to know. Who?

His manager, Teresa? I'd watched her argue with Joey

from my position on the stage, and it was her card stapled to the outside of the bag.

Joey himself? If he was guilty, he'd want to throw suspicion elsewhere, and he knew exactly who this bra would implicate.

Chryssinda? She couldn't have known I saw her and Joey that very first day, but had she stuffed the bra into this bag in order to dispose of it?

Or was there someone else, someone completely different, who I was overlooking?

I had no idea how long this bag had been waiting for me at Will Call. My appointment with Joey's had been yesterday morning, the day after Lydia's body had been found. What if someone had expected me to come across this last night when I left the show? Would I have put two and two together fast enough to keep Chryssinda from getting hurt?

I couldn't just sit there and think about the implications of not checking Will Call until today. I also couldn't determine who was behind the gesture. I dropped onto the bed and closed my eyes. Something was off.

Room service arrived just about the same time Nick did, conveniently canceling out my need to explain two empty bowls of mac and gruyere while allowing me to look considerate. I doubted Nick would have bought any explanation I came up with after my confession this morning. Still, it was nice not to worry.

I thanked Fred, signed the room service slip, and

moved the cart to the foot of the bed. Nick stood next to it, staring at the assortment of panties strewn across the comforter. Aside from the cone bra, I'd come home with bikinis, briefs, thongs, and G-strings. Nick didn't speak for a while, and I misunderstood his concern.

"They're vendor samples," I said. "I worked today. Like, work-worked. I made a ton of contacts for Tradava, and most of the booths, when they heard I was shopping for new vendors for a department store, sent me off with a gift."

"Standard trade show behavior," Nick said.

"Yes."

"Are you planning on keeping them?"

"Probably."

"Maybe you should try them on. See which ones you like. I could help you decide."

I looked from Nick's face to the panties on the bed and back to Nick's face. He picked up a black G-string and dangled it from his finger.

"I'm pretty sure I'm not going to like that pair," I said. I took the sliver of elastic from his hand and balled it up like a cocktail napkin. "I generally like my panties to leave a little something to the imagination."

He smiled. "Like these?" He held up a pair of white cotton granny panties.

"There's probably a happy medium." (If I didn't stop with the mac and cheese, I'd need a happy large.) "Speaking of mac and cheese, we should eat before the food gets cold."

"We weren't speaking of mac and cheese," he said.

"Oh, I guess that was in my head."

Nick washed his hands while I swept the mound of panties out of the way. We ate. Between bites, he told me about his day babysitting Marc (seven casinos, two emotional breakdowns, three hundred thousand dollars, zero hookers) and I told him about finding Chryssinda unconscious in Joey's booth and the cone bra that someone had left at Will Call under my name.

"I can't help but circle back around to Joey. He stands to gain the most from that distasteful photo that was in the paper. So much of what I know points to Joey, but then there's the pages missing from the wedding guestbook, and that has nothing to do with the lingerie show." I finished off my last bite and set down my fork. "It doesn't add up."

"I hate to say it, but you're right. If we hadn't spoken to the chaplain himself, then everything about Lydia's death would point to the lingerie fair and Joey. That's the angle that's being played out in the news. Tragic death of lingerie model during Intimate Mode Week."

"They still haven't ruled her death suspicious or come out with a cause of death, have they?"

"No. So far the press is letting it read, unofficially, like a suicide. People move on to new things so quickly, Lydia's death is already old news."

"But if the police aren't releasing a cause of death or a definitive statement of suicide, then they still aren't sure about what happened."

"That's what it looks like." Nick scooped up the last of the mac and cheese, swallowed, and set down his fork too.

"There's only one thing to do," I said.

"I know."

I studied Nick's face, not sure how he was going to feel about going to the source. I waited several seconds to give him a chance to speak, just in case his idea was more along the lines of "walk away," or "leave things to the police" or "trade in our plane tickets and cut our trip short." When he didn't speak, I did.

"You know I'm saying we need to talk to Marc, right? Flat-out ask him about the wedding?"

Nick looked surprised. "That's what you meant?"

"Yes. What did you think I meant?"

"I thought you were going to suggest we order more food."

———

WE STOOD SIDE by side in front of Marc Rico's hotel room. Judging from the lack of doors on the left and right side of it, took up more space than four of our Napoleon rooms put together. Marc answered my knock in a paisley silk robe with MR monogrammed on it over a white T-shirt and gray silk pajama bottoms. He held a tumbler of ice and something amber.

"Sammie, Nick. Nice surprise," he said. His eyes were

red-rimmed, and his speech was slow—not quite slurred, but controlled.

I glanced at Nick, who seemed unfazed by Marc's condition.

"Come on in. Can I get you something from the bar?"

"Sure," Nick said. He put his hand on the small of my back and guided me inside.

Marc's room was posh. Heavy burgundy curtains framed a window that provided a view of the strip. Sheer white fabric diffused the light, casting a filmy glow over the furniture. The bed was unmade, but otherwise, the room was immaculate. I assumed being wealthy and temporarily living in a hotel was a good combination for someone in Marc's current state.

Which wasn't a particularly cheerful one, now that I stopped to think about it. No matter what the reality was about Lydia, Marc had been having a hard time of things ever since I'd met him. The tragedy of someone working through this amount of emotional pain and not being able to say or do anything about it crushed me. While Nick poured two glasses of wine, I gave Marc an unexpected hug. He hesitated only a moment before hugging back.

"I'm so sorry for your loss," I said. "I don't know if I've said that yet. This whole trip, everything, it has to be hard on you."

Marc slowly pulled away from me. "I need to tell you something. Both of you. Nick, you're one of my oldest friends. I trust you. I've been holding onto a secret that's tearing me apart."

"Sit down," Nick said.

He led Marc to the corner of the bed. Nick and I sat across from him on the velvet loveseat.

"It's going to take time, man," he said. "You can't rush your emotions." He glanced at the glass in Marc's hand. "You can try to forget them for a little bit, but that's not going to help you long term."

I leaned forward and took Marc's hand. "Marc, no matter what happened to Lydia, she died knowing you loved her."

"No, she didn't," he said. He stared into his glass.

Nick and I looked at each other. I felt my face draw into a *what?* expression which Nick met with an *I-have-no-idea* shrug.

Marc poured the rest of his drink down his throat and looked up at us. "I was never going to marry Lydia. She was a diversion to keep the press from finding out the truth."

"Which was what?" I asked.

"My fiancée was Chryssinda. All along, it's been Chryssinda. We've gone out of our way to keep it a secret, but somebody knows. Somebody who wants to destroy me killed the wrong woman."

26

DEATH THREATS

I put my hand on Nick's arm as a signal not to say anything, and he pressed his thigh sideways in response. I could get used to this nonverbal communication thing.

Marc continued. "Chryssie and I agreed it was best to keep things quiet until it was official. I've had—there's been—I've gotten some death threats. The police know about them, and they're working on tracking down the source. I probably wouldn't have taken them seriously, but with Chryssinda in my life, I didn't want to take any chances."

As Marc spoke, my mind raced. Now I understood why Marc had jumped the gun and paid off another couple to take their spot—because keeping his engagement secret was driving him crazy. Or perhaps it was Chryssinda who'd suggested they bump up the timetable. It explained the tension I'd gleaned from Chaplain Rick. There *had* been trouble surrounding

Marc and his bride—she just wasn't the bride I'd thought her to be.

The torn pages from the wedding guestbook? Still working that out.

"What kind of threats are we talking about?" I asked. I felt Nick's eyes on me, but I didn't look at him.

"They started out as phone calls. 'I'm going to destroy you,' and 'you'll pay for what you did.' Never a message. Only when I was physically on the call. Never my cell, so there was no way to see which cell towers were pinged or isolate the physical location of the caller. There's a certain amount of BS you have to accept when you get to my level. I ignored it as long as I could."

"Someone called you and said they were going to destroy you, and you ignored it?" I asked.

"As far as threats go, these were relatively vague. Who can destroy me? One phone call and a helicopter full of security agents lands on the roof. I've got loyal and highly paid experts on my payroll monitoring my money and investments. I make my own business decisions, green light or red light, and I stand by them. I've always lived a public life, and that's how I want it."

"But all that changed when you met Chryssinda."

He nodded. "Chryssie was different. She was a smart, confident woman. She never asked me for anything. She insisted on a prenup, not the other way around. She had her own money."

"If she had money, why did she work as an escort?"

Marc didn't flinch at my slightly inappropriate

question. "She enjoyed a certain lifestyle, and the service put her in the company of men who enjoyed those things too."

"And it doesn't bother you that she was with—you know—others?"

"Chryssinda is twenty-three. I'm forty. I've probably had more action than she has. That's reality. She's uninhibited and loves her body. I won't pretend the sex isn't great, but what I love is that she understands the pressures that come with my life and expects nothing. I never felt like she was a gold digger."

I glanced at Nick to see what he was thinking. He hadn't said anything since Marc's big confession, and while Nick's silence allowed me the freedom to ask questions that could be perceived as innocent, I couldn't ignore the tension coming from him. He kept his eyes on Marc and his thigh pressed against mine. Enough to tell me to keep going.

At least I was pretty sure that's what his thigh pressure meant. Maybe he was doing isometric exercises to work off the mac and cheese.

"Marc, everything you told us about Lydia, about how you met her, were you talking about Chryssinda?"

Marc's smile didn't reach his eyes. "We had to keep our relationship quiet. Lydia and Chryssie were friends from modeling, so when Chryssie and I wanted to make things official, we came up with the plan to have Lydia pose as the beard. Lydia's career started to take off, and all sorts of rumors come with that. I figured we could leak the fake story and let the tabloids run with it. In time, I'd let one of my media channels do some fact checking and expose the gossip rags for what they are."

"And make money off your cover story with your own companies," I added.

"Kidd!" Nick exclaimed.

"She's right," Marc countered.

"See?" That was me.

Marc continued. "I have to play that way, Nick. Especially when I have people coming after me. It's eat or be eaten." He stood up and refilled his glass. "It's why Chryssie kept her hotel reservation at Flush even though she mostly stays here with me. If someone's watching her, I want to know. That's why security escorted us out of The Heart Club when we got drunk. They were paid to protect Chryssie and Lydia, and our actions put the women at risk. I handle my own problems. I thought I could smoke out whoever is coming after me. I was wrong. Lydia's dead, and Chryssie won't even return my calls."

He didn't know. Marc and Chryssinda had kept their relationship so quiet that he didn't even know she was at the local hospital after being found unconscious. Detective Marbury had left with Joey Cheeks. He probably didn't know to notify Marc, and it twisted my gut to have to cause him additional pain.

"Marc, Chryssinda isn't avoiding you. She's in the hospital. I went to the lingerie show early today, and I found her. Unconscious. She was taken away for emergency treatment. I don't know which hospital, but it should be easy enough to find out. Detective Marbury was there."

The billionaire jumped up from the bed and stalked to the hotel phone. "Get me the police," he said to whoever answered. He kept his back to us while he waited to be connected.

I turned to Nick. "He couldn't know," I said. "Nobody would have known to tell him. The only other people who know the truth are Chaplain Rick, Irene, and Chryssinda."

"And the couple who he paid off to take their place," Nick said.

"But do they know who he is? Or did they just accept cash from a rich stranger who made it worth their while to wait a day?" I thought for a second. "Marc's rich, but it's not like he's a Kardashian. Nobody knows who he is. You two were pretty toasted on Saturday night, and nobody treated him like a celebrity. You both said you don't remember a lot of what happened. Add in Marc and Chryssinda's spontaneous wedding, and his guard was probably down. If someone was following him, they could very easily have gotten to him—or gotten to her to get to him."

"If someone has it in for Marc, they're not going to stop at Lydia and Chryssinda," he said. "Marc needs a friend right now, and I'm all he has. I don't want to see him dive into a bottle that he can't climb out of." He cupped the side of my face and gave me a tender kiss.

"Leaving you alone is the last thing I want right now, but I don't think I should leave Marc alone tonight either."

For all the times I'd put friendship before my job, my safety, and my common sense, it warmed my heart to see Nick do it, too. I put my hand on top of his. "I understand. I'll be here when you need me."

Marc got off the phone. "She's at the Las Vegas Memorial Hospital," he said.

Nick stood up. "Come on. I'll go with you."

Marc turned to me. "Sammie, will you—can you stay at the hotel?" he asked. "I'll tell the front desk to direct my calls to your room. In case there's news, I want someone to be here to answer the phone."

"Sure. Go. I'll call you if I hear anything."

It was closing in on eight o'clock, and visiting hours at the hospital ended at nine. Marc left us in the living room portion of his massive hotel suite while he changed into a less Hugh Hefner outfit. I said goodnight to Nick and sent the two men on their way.

Whether it was Nick's act of friendship toward Marc, or the annoying fact that the closest friend I had in Las Vegas was Amanda Ries, I was homesick. I'd been out of Ribbon for four days, and I missed my friends, my cat, and my routine. I missed hoagies and pizza and pretzels. There was nothing wrong with a menu that featured twenty-two versions of mac and cheese, but sometimes you want the blue box of Kraft with the electric-yellow powder.

I flopped on the bed and called Eddie.

"Hey, dude," I said when he answered.

"Hey." There was a pause. "Are you in trouble?"

"Not right now."

"Are you about to get married?"

"Not right now," I repeated.

"Okay, good. I'm on my way out. Logan's fine, and your tomato plant hasn't died yet. Tell me again why you have a tomato plant?"

"It's the one vegetable that goes in everything I like: pizza, spaghetti sauce, meatball sandwiches, and hoagies."

"You get your hoagies without tomatoes. Something about the bread getting soggy."

"Whatever," I said.

"Listen, can I call you tomorrow? I'm on my way to a fundraiser at the skateboard park."

"Sure," I said, though it was obvious I was lying.

He hesitated. "Are you sure you're not being held at gunpoint by a murderer?"

"I'm sure. Go have fun." I paused, then added, "That skateboard park holds a lot of memories. I'll donate fifty dollars to the cause."

———

IF I WERE AT HOME, I'd probably be hanging out with Nick and his dad, who had moved in with him after breaking his hip last year. If I weren't with Nick, I'd be with Eddie. If I weren't with Eddie, I'd be with Logan.

And if Logan was in one of his moods where he'd rather spend time with the catnip mouse, then I'd do my laundry. Nobody likes dirty laundry, but calling hotel services to do the job for me lacked the satisfaction of doing a couple of loads myself. Even the thought of mac and cheese didn't perk me up. I ordered ice cream instead.

I was bored. I went to my room and sorted the panty samples into piles: Yes, and Heck No. About twenty minutes later, (time killed trying to understand a black lace pair that turned out to be crotchless), there was a knock on the door. Expecting room service, I peeked through the peephole and saw two buxom women in low-cut evening dresses.

I opened the door. "Can I help you?"

"Hi," said the woman on the left. She wore a purple jersey dress that clung to everything she had. The hotel hadn't seemed particularly cold, but she was perky. "I'm Kristin. This is Sue Ellen. We heard you were asking around about some company tonight?"

"No, I'm just waiting for room service."

Sue Ellen, a chocolate brunette in emerald green, laughed. "Sure, you can call us room service."

"No, I mean room service-room service. Food. I think maybe you have the wrong room."

The women looked at each other. "Can you believe this?" Kristin asked Sue Ellen. "He said it's a no-brainer. He said it would be worth our while. I turned down two other dates for this gig."

I blame the distraction of homesickness and a bounty of panties for being obtuse. Because the conclusion that would have seemed obvious to almost anybody else paying attention took embarrassingly long for me to reach.

The women in front of me were "escorts."

27

PROFESSIONALS

"Ladies," I said politely, "I think I know how this happened. Come on in."

They looked at each other, shrugged, and entered.

I eased the door shut behind them. "My fiancé was asking around about escort services—"

Sue Ellen looked at Kristin. "Oooh, this might be fun after all."

"No," I said. "He wasn't calling for himself. He was calling for me."

Kristin smiled. "Honey, there's no shame in that. We're professionals."

"No!" I said again, this time taking a step backward. "Look, it was a misunderstanding. Nick and I get the job done with just the two of us. Neither one of us wanted to hire company. I mean no disrespect because I'm sure you're both very good at what you do."

Sue Ellen looked confused. "Who's Nick?"

"My fiancé. The one who was asking around about your services."

"Honey, if you know he was asking about us, then what's the problem?" She looked past me into the suite. "Where is this Nick?"

There was a knock on the door. "Room service," said a male voice.

Kristin fluffed her already-bouncy blond hair. "Role playing! How fun!"

I pulled the door open and greeted Fred. "No mac and cheese tonight?" he asked. "You still haven't tried number thirteen and number twenty."

I took the black folio, filled out the tip, and signed the bill to the room. "I was in the mood for something different."

Fred looked at Kristin and Sue Ellen. "I can see that."

I handed the folio back to Fred and grabbed the cart. "I'll take it from here." I shut the door as quickly as I could. If only I'd called hotel services to wash my clothes, this would have gone completely differently. Hotel services didn't know me. Seeing two seductively attired women in my room after eight on a Tuesday might not have appeared all that suspicious to them.

Who was I kidding?

I turned back to the ladies. "Kristin, Sue Ellen, I am sorry. Like I said, my fiancé was asking around about your services for a friend. I'm not making that up. One of his friends met his wife through a company like yours, and Nick was acting on his friend's behalf. There's no job here, not that there's anything wrong with your work, just that I don't need your services."

"Well, that's just great," Sue Ellen said. She tossed her gold handbag on the love seat and dropped down next to it. "I wasted two hours getting ready for this."

Kristin sat down next to her. "We could call the office and see if the boss man has any last-minute gigs? Or we could cruise the casino."

"What do you think we're going to shake loose on a Tuesday?" Sue Ellen asked.

"Fine, I'll call the office." Kristin opened her silver handbag (the ladies had paid attention to their styles while preparing for the evening, I had to give them that) and pulled out her phone. She stood up and walked to the window, revealing the open back to her purple gown and the lack of bra strap. Now I understood where the perkiness came from: surgery.

"It's Kristin," she said. "You messed up big time, Jack. Sue Ellen and I did what you said, but there isn't any job here." She waited a couple of seconds then glanced at Sue Ellen, who crossed her arms over her generous chest. "I'm telling you, you're wrong. Drop the phony accent and give me another address. It's early enough that the night doesn't have to be a total bust." She snapped her fingers at me, pointed to the notepad on the table, and pantomimed writing something down. I handed her the tablet and the pen, and she scribbled on the paper. When she hung up, she gave the notepad to Sue Ellen.

Sue Ellen glanced at the tablet and looked up. "He

wants us to go to the other end of the strip? I'm sorry. I'm not in the mood to mingle with tourists on the Deuce."

Kristin turned back to me. "Are you sure you don't want company?"

I wanted company, just not that kind of company. "I'm sorry. I'm pretty traditional."

Kristin slid her index finger under the elastic waistband on the crotchless panties on the bedspread and dangled them in front of me. "You sure about that?"

I felt my face flush. "Those are samples from the lingerie show. Designers give buyers presents, and this was today's haul."

I'd said the magic words. Both women dropped the seductress act.

"You're a lingerie buyer?"

"Can you get us samples?"

"Forget samples. Can you get us a job?"

"That would be so much better than working for Pepe Le Pew."

"Hallelujah, sister." They high fived. "I would love some regular hours."

I looked at the two of them: two women who had shown up expecting something very different from the night they'd had. They didn't seem all that disappointed. I had no idea what life decisions had led them to their current line of work. They were the same decisions that had led Chryssinda to work as an escort, and Chryssinda had met Marc, the love of her life. In a twisted way, Chryssinda had happened upon a fairy tale ending—at the expense of her friend Lydia's life. I guess even fairy tale endings are bittersweet.

It struck me that Kristin and Sue Ellen were here because Nick had been asking about high-priced escort services, and he'd done that because he wanted to find out more about Lydia. We now knew the escort business was a dead end because Lydia had never worked for the escort service, Chryssinda had.

Except now, I didn't know if it *was* a dead end. "Did either of you know Chryssinda Sykes?"

"Chryssie?" Kristin said. "I heard about her, but I don't know her. She left before I started." She turned to Sue Ellen. "You know who she means, right? 'Big Shoes.' That's what the boss man calls her."

"Oh, sure," Sue Ellen said. "Whatever happened to her?"

They looked at me. "She's out of the business," I said tactfully. "She had an accident earlier today and is in the hospital. Nick took his friend to see her. Marc was pretty upset when he found out."

At the mention of Marc's name, Sue Ellen's head snapped to attention. "Marc? You don't mean Marc Rico, do you?"

"Yes. How'd you know that?"

The two women looked at each other again. "That's who we were hired to entertain."

The room was in Marc's name. And Marc had told the front desk to direct his calls to my room. Whoever had sent the ladies to the hotel had gotten our identities confused. And then a couple of little details clicked into place, and I surprised myself with an unexpected conclusion.

"When you called your office, you referred to somebody as Jack. Was that a throwaway like 'honey' or 'babe'?"

The ladies looked at each other and shrugged. "No, that's the boss man's name," Kristin said. And when Sue Ellen jumped in, she confirmed my suspicions.

"He pretends to be French because he thinks the hotel guests like it. Honestly, the only thing French about Pepe Le Pew is that he stinks."

"Jacques, the hotel concierge, is Jack, your boss?" I said.

"Yeah, that's him," Kristin said.

"Ladies, I changed my mind about wanting some company tonight. How about we order some room service—on me—and have a nice, long chat?"

28

SAMANTHA FOOD

I FLUSHED THE NOW-MELTED ICE CREAM DOWN THE TOILET and placed a new room service order. In addition to three orders of lobster mac and cheese, I ordered Samantha-food from the children's menu: chicken fingers, French fries, and pizza. I added three bottles of champagne. I couldn't afford to pay the ladies their regular rate, but that didn't mean I couldn't treat them in the style they'd become accustomed to. (The chicken fingers were for me.)

I graciously told them to take whichever panties they wanted from the assortment on the bed and provided empty goodie bags for them to carry their swag. While they sorted through the swag, I called the one person I never, ever, *ever* thought I'd invite to hang out with me.

"Hi Amanda, it's Samantha," I said. "Nick and Marc are at the hospital with Chryssinda. I made some new friends, and I thought maybe, if you weren't busy tonight, you might want to join us?"

The phone was silent for so long I thought the call had dropped. "Hello? Amanda? Are you there?"

"I'm here." She cleared her throat. "Sure. I'll be there in about fifteen minutes."

"Hey," I said, catching her before she hung up. "Bring the suit I spilled soda on today. I'll call hotel services and have it laundered."

I hung up, feeling all kinds of mature. In one night I'd uncovered a solid lead in Jacques, made friends with two call girls, and invited Amanda to hang out. By the time I got back home to Ribbon, Eddie wasn't even going to recognize me.

———

AMANDA ARRIVED ABOUT the same time as the room service cart. Fred popped the champagne while I signed the bill. I made brief introductions ("This is Amanda. She's a lingerie designer. Amanda, this is Kristin and Sue Ellen. They also work in lingerie.") After a lightning round of handshakes and hugs, we settled in for some good, old-fashioned girl talk.

"Tell me what you know about Jacques," I said. "Jack. Pepe le Pew. I don't care what you call him, I want to know whatever you can tell me."

"Sure," Kristin said. Both women had kicked off their heels and now padded around in bare feet. I'd politely offered sweatshirts and had been surprised when both accepted. Kristin wore my *I got tied up in Ribbon!* one and Sue Ellen wore Nick's I-FAD hoodie. Amanda wore a long-sleeved black T-shirt, skinny jeans, and pale-pink loafers. Aside from an ill-advised foray into space-age designs for a recent runway show, her personal style had always trended toward classic.

"Jack manages a stable of ten ladies," Kristin said.

"Like models?" Amanda asked innocently. "I need to hire a couple of models for the show tomorrow."

Kristin, Sue Ellen, and I exchanged glances. "Sue Ellen, why don't you and Amanda go"—I glanced around—"over there and talk about that? You can probably work something out, right?"

"Sure," Sue Ellen said. She grabbed a plate of fries and a bottle of champagne. Amanda followed her.

"Back to Jacques," I said to Kristin. "He's your 'manager,' right?"

"Yeah. There's no actual office, but his job here lets him know when there's a guest who fits a certain profile. Some of the men ask him to arrange dates. That's what it is, you know. We get paid for our time. Anything other than time is extra. Like ordering side dishes a la carte."

"Of course," I said immediately. "I was just wondering about how Jacques connects you with clients. Like tonight. You said you heard I was asking around about your services, and it's true, my fiancé was asking some questions, but he got picked up for suspicion of solicitation—"

"He what? Oh, honey, if he got picked up, then he wasn't asking the right questions!" She doubled over in laughter and took another swig from her champagne flute.

I bit into the last chicken finger. While I chewed, I considered that. "Nick probably had no idea Jacques was your pim—manager," I quickly corrected. "I bet he asked Jacques, who is the hotel concierge, a couple of discreet questions, and Jacques set him up."

I couldn't believe I'd never asked Nick who he'd talked to about escort services, but this made sense. It also made me even more suspicious about the man who knew our whereabouts the entire time we'd been at the hotel. Jacques could easily queue up the room tab and see what I ate, when I left, and where I was.

Except, now that we were on Marc's tab, was it all the same? I didn't know.

"Kristin, you said Jacques sent you up here to entertain Marc Rico. What did Jacques say when you called him tonight? Was he surprised Marc wasn't here?"

"He was pretty insistent that I was wrong. He said he knew Marc was in here because there'd been activity on his bill."

"That was me. My room is under Marc's name. Jacques probably doesn't know which charges are mine and which charges are Marc's."

Which meant all this time, Jacques had been watching Marc's hotel room bill. He probably did the same thing for other big spenders and made arrangements on the side. Kristin and Sue Ellen hadn't been hired. They'd been sent here.

"How were you going to get paid tonight?" I asked. "If Marc didn't know you were coming, did you expect him to have money? Or to know why you were here? How does it work?"

"We get paid on the back end," Kristin said. "Jacques charges our companionship to the room."

I couldn't believe it. Jacques was running an under-the-table "escort" ring using the hotel's books to make it all appear legitimate! If a guest questioned his bill, Jacques would have blackmail material to keep things quiet. And while I knew he knew Chryssinda and would have likely known about her relationship with Marc, if he'd been getting paid for her time with Marc in the dating days, he would have been looking at a significant loss of income after the two of them married.

He'd also have a whole lot to lose if Lydia Moss—merely posing as one of his stable—had anything to say to the press, or if one of Marc's media companies exposed Jacques' operation.

But Lydia was becoming more known in the modeling industry every day. Her make-believe background story would easily be exposed as gossip, but would she risk her career by exposing Jacques' operation to the press? Or had Chryssinda promised to handle that angle? Did Lydia have it in her to blackmail any of the parties involved?

Jacques would lose more than his job if anyone found

out what business he'd been conducting under the guise of "concierge," and right now, Chryssinda was a loose end.

I didn't yet understand how he could have gotten to her at the lingerie fair, but I could think of one very good reason Jacques had arranged for Kristin and Sue Ellen to entertain Marc Rico tonight—to keep Marc away from Chryssinda so Jacques could finish what he'd started.

29

BEATS GIVING BACK RUBS

"When you called Jacques, was he working the front desk?" I asked Kristin.

"No, Tuesdays are his night off."

"Do you know where he's at?"

"He said he had some unexpected business leads to follow up on."

A rush of adrenaline surged through me. I grabbed my phone from the nightstand and called Nick. The call rang several times and then went to voicemail. I hung up and tried again. This time I left a message. "Nick, it's Samantha. I just found out Jacques, the concierge, is the one running the escort service where Chryssinda worked. I think he might be on his way to the hospital to hurt her. If you see him, alert security."

I hung up and set my phone on the nightstand. When I turned around, Kristin stood in front of me. She'd taken off my sweatshirt and set it on the bed. "Who did you just call?"

"Nick. He's with Marc. They're with Chryssinda."

"Why do you think Jacques is going to hurt Chryssinda? She doesn't work for him anymore. She quit a couple of months ago."

"He's probably mad at her. He lost a lot of money when she quit, right? You said he calls her 'Big Shoes.' That's because she brought in big clients, right? I mean, Marc's a whale. Isn't that the lingo?"

"Jacques calls Chryssinda 'Big Shoes' because she wears a size eleven. She bought her own clothes, and he didn't like that because he couldn't hold it over her head that he invested in her. He was happy when she quit because she always told us to stand up to him and call our own shots. All he did for us was coordinate meetings. She worked when she wanted to, and he saw her modeling career as a conflict of interest. This was a side gig for her."

"But Jacques wanted her out of the picture. He had to have. And when he found out her friend was pretending to work for him to throw the media scent off Chryssinda and Marc, he killed her friend."

Even as I said it, I felt the air fizzle out of my suspicions. Kristin stepped away from me. "Jacques isn't a killer," she said. "He's an opportunist, sure, but you better watch what you say about him. He might be a putz with a fake accent, but a lot of people in this hotel rely on him for special requests, and he delivers. My kids have healthcare because of the work he does. If he heard what you're saying, you'd be out on the street."

I recognized Kristin's blind faith in Jacques' innocence. I'd felt that way myself when people I knew were suspected of crimes. But just because I recognized it didn't mean I was willing to write off my suspicions. Believing Jacques to be innocent didn't necessarily make it so.

Sue Ellen and Amanda had stopped talking, and Sue Ellen joined Kristin. She pulled Nick's I-FAD sweatshirt off and tossed it on the bed. "I think maybe we've worn out our welcome."

"No, ladies, listen." I put my hand out and grabbed Kristin's wrist. "Please understand. The day after I arrived in Las Vegas, I found a woman's body. I think she was murdered. And a couple of days after that, her friend was found unconscious. I don't know who's behind it or why, and that's making me a little crazy."

Kristin looked at my hand on her wrist, and I let go.

"I'm in an unfamiliar town where I have two friends: Nick and Amanda." I glanced at Amanda. "I'm known for jumping to conclusions. Let's keep what I said between us girls and call it a night."

Kristin and Sue Ellen looked at each other. "I don't know," Kristin said. "Jacques will probably make tonight worth our while if we tell him what she said."

These ladies were no dummies. "Hold up. You said Jacques bills your services to the room, right?"

"Yeah. So?"

"Tell him it was a misunderstanding and we worked everything out. Tell him you stayed here. Tell him whatever it is you tell him after you do whatever it is you do."

The ladies looked at each other again. Sue Ellen shrugged. "What the heck. Beats giving back rubs."

———

I SENT THE LADIES on their way and locked the door behind them. I'd explain the charges to Nick and Marc when the time came. Despite my explanation of my actions to the women, I kept Jacques on my suspect list. He had opportunity and a possible motive. Marc would be the best person to tell me about his standing relationship with Jacques.

I texted Nick, told him to disregard my voicemail, and immediately followed it up with another saying to not disregard it completely, but that I lacked evidence to support my suspicions. I considered calling the police, but what would I tell them? The only thing I'd confirmed for sure was that Jacques used a fake accent. Anybody who'd ever seen a Pink Panther movie would have recognized that.

I set the various plates on the room service cart and pushed the cart into the hallway. We'd kicked all three bottles of champagne, but I hadn't even finished a glass. I checked the minibar, pulled out two splits, and handed one to Amanda.

"We might as well keep the party going."

Amanda took the bottle and rested it on her thigh. "You just called me your friend. Are we?"

I considered the question. "We're not *not* friends. I guess it was always just easier to not like you than to like you, because if I liked you I'd have to accept your place in Nick's life."

She peeled the foil from her bottle and popped the cork. "Trust me, accepting you hasn't been a walk in the park either."

I'd never considered that, and the thought made me smile. I opened my bottle, we filled our glasses, and clinked.

Hey, what happens in Vegas stays in Vegas, right?

We each finished a glass and poured another. I took a much-needed bathroom break and came back to find Amanda standing by the window, staring out at the view of the strip.

"Is everything okay?" I asked her.

She didn't answer right way. When she finally did speak, it wasn't what I expected. "What did Nick tell you about Pamela's death?"

"Pamela? Your college roommate?" I thought about the conversation Nick and I had while he was hung over after his Vegas bender with Marc. It had been along the lines of just-the-facts, but I'd gotten the gist of it. "He said he and Pamela broke up, and she almost immediately started dating Marc. When he tired of her, she begged

Nick to take her back, and he didn't. She killed herself, and a part of him feels guilty."

"Did he say why he feels guilty?" Amanda asked.

"Nick's a smart guy. I don't think he regrets not reconciling with Pamela after she left him, but I do think he thinks he should have seen she was troubled and maybe gotten her help."

Amanda returned to her chair. She crossed and recrossed her legs several times, as if the subject made her uncomfortable and she couldn't relax. The incident had happened a long time ago, but clearly it was as fresh in Amanda's mind as it was in Nick's.

"Why did Lydia's death remind you of Pamela? You told Nick you thought I could help. What did you mean?"

"Lydia's death looked like a suicide, but the paper said the medical examiner hadn't released the cause of death. That's what happened with Pamela at first. Even though it looked like suicide with her mental state and overdose, there were questions and an ensuing investigation."

"But it was ruled a suicide in the end?"

"Yes," Amanda said.

"How do you know all this? I know you were her roommate, but you never seemed all that interested in criminal investigation, and you don't talk about her like you two were close," I said.

Amanda sighed. "Pamela and I were roommates matched by the computer. We didn't have much in common, but when you're put in a close living situation like that, you become friends. I can't explain it, but that's how it was. I knew things about her that nobody else knew because we shared a room. You can only hide so much when you share a twenty-foot space with another person."

"What does any of this have to do with Lydia? Right now, the only connection I see is that both women were connected to Marc. But you're talking about something that happened a long time ago."

Amanda didn't seem to find it as odd as I did. "We all attended I-FAD."

And then it dawned on me that it wasn't a coincidence. That Nick joining me in Las Vegas wasn't simply a spontaneous getaway, that Amanda entering the lingerie market wasn't a random choice. That Marc wasn't just in Las Vegas to get married. I felt my eyes move back and forth as pieces of conversations that I'd heard from the moment I stepped foot into the hotel dropped into corresponding places like a game of Tetris.

"Nick told me Marc is your financial backer. Your company was ruined. You knew Marc from college, and you reached out to him for funding. Lydia said something about that—about how opportunistic designers came out of the woodwork to get at his money. I thought she was talking about Nick because he was with Marc at the time, but she was talking about you. Am I right?"

"You're not wrong," she said.

"And instead of investing in your company, he gave you a job."

"No, he bought my company and let me stay on as an

advisor. He thought it was wise for me to go into a niche category that I had no connection to while we rebuilt my brand, and he pulled strings to get me into the Intimate Mode show."

It was solid advice, and Amanda was smart to have turned to someone who knew what he was talking about. "You talked to Marc about Nick's financial trouble too, didn't you?"

She nodded. "After Marc bought my company, I told him about Nick's situation. He wanted to talk to Nick about possible opportunities. I didn't think Nick would even consider it, but I told Nick I wanted him to meet my new investor. I didn't tell him who it was until after he found out Marc was in Vegas."

"We ran into Marc when we checked in. Nick seemed surprised by Marc being here."

"He would have been. I planned to have Marc and Nick meet at Flush. Yesterday when you left in my sample robe and I said I had an appointment—that was Marc. I didn't think it was a good idea for him to find out what you did or that I was involved."

"When Nick agreed to come to Vegas with me, he wanted to get away from his recent problems, but seeing Marc reminded him of old problems." I started to understand why Nick had acted so strange that very first day and why he said Marc Rico was the last person he wanted to owe. Nick had narrowly missed owing some very bad people. It would be hard enough for him to accept help rebuilding, but help coming from Marc would have reminded him too much of the past.

"Nick came to Vegas to spend time with you. When you asked him, he thought maybe you had something else in mind." She sang the first four notes—*da dum de dum*—of the wedding march. "Meeting with investors wasn't his priority."

"But right after we checked into the hotel he went off with Marc."

"Nick was mad. At Marc, at me, at all of us. He might have thought you were in on it too."

"He thought I had something to do with Marc meeting us in the lobby?"

She shrugged. "You like to solve problems. If Marc invested in Nick's company, that would be a problem solved. But Nick wanted time with you. He didn't want any interruptions. I kept prodding him to meet with my investor, and when he realized that investor was Marc, he felt trapped. When he found out Marc was getting married, Nick felt like a fool for thinking it was all about him."

30

AN ODDLY BONDING MOMENT

At least I now knew Nick hadn't lied to me. When I'd first told him about the lingerie show in Las Vegas, he asked if I wanted company. He joked about having a flexible schedule, and he said there would be possible leads for him at the accessory shows. All true. It wasn't like Nick knew everything about my life, so I had no reason to know every detail about his.

"Tell me how you reconnected with Marc," I said.

"You know I had business trouble." It was a statement, not a question.

Yes, I knew. It was over a year ago. An arsonist had targeted Amanda's runway show. I'd volunteered to help her before Nick's and my relationship hit some speed bumps. I would have come out of the situation feeling far superior to Amanda in terms of business acumen and high road taking, but she'd seen me in my underwear, and that was kind of an equalizer.

But all things considered, an entire convention center of industry professionals had seen me in my underwear now, so that shaved the edge off Amanda's high ground.

"I took a year off," she said. "I applied for a teaching position at I-FAD and sent out resumes to everybody I knew on LinkedIn. Honestly, I thought I was done with the fashion business. Even if I had something creative left to say, my name was a joke. Why would anybody pay attention to me?"

"Did you go to Marc, or did he come to you?"

"I saw his name in the alumni magazine. I-FAD is known for being a design school, but Marc is one of our more successful graduates from the business side. The current faculty wants to use his success to recruit more candidates for that major, so there was a profile on him. There I was, sitting in my living room in my underwear, asking the universe for a sign. The mail arrived, and inside was the magazine with that profile."

I showed great restraint by not saying a word. I'd been known to look for signs on occasion, so anything I said would have had a pot/kettle/black feeling.

"You called Marc and set up a meeting," I said.

Amanda's face softened, and I realized she'd been expecting the very comment I'd kept in reserve. It was an oddly bonding moment.

"I reached out to congratulate him on the article. He'd heard about my business trouble. The next day, he called and said he may have an opportunity for me and did I want to meet to talk?"

"That fast?"

"I asked the universe for a sign. It's not like I was in a position to ignore him. Even if I didn't want the job, I probably would have asked him for a loan so I could get caught up on my bills and not have credit problems on top of everything else."

I hadn't spent much time thinking about Amanda's life after her troubles. I'll admit, I'm the center of my own universe. The problems I have take center stage, and the problems I get mixed up in tend to override everything else going on around me. And helping Amanda had led to my own set of problems.

I'd been hospitalized (talk about signs). When I recovered, I vowed to take control of my life. I accepted a job at a local start-up e-zine, which had been acquired by Tradava Department Stores, thus giving me the very financial stability I'd sought when I first moved back to Ribbon. I pushed Amanda out of my mind to keep my eyes on my own paper, and enough had happened since then that I'd never stopped to think about the damage done to her life. Did that make me a bad person? I didn't think so. But it did make me reconsider any snap judgments over the decisions she'd made.

Amanda was the sort of woman to whom it appeared things came easily. She had naturally sleek and straight hair while I had curls that I fought to tame. She had the figure of a model pre-body positive movement, while I had sandwich rolls around my waist. She had her name on the inside label of the clothes in the fashion magazines I read. The closest I'd come to having my name on a designer label was when my mom wrote "S. KIDD" on the elastic inside my Carter's cotton briefs.

I'd almost lost everything when I first moved to Ribbon. And Nick had lost everything when his showroom manager had been murdered. But watching Amanda lose everything had taught me a valuable lesson. We are all in control of our own lives, and it's our responsibility to look out for ourselves. It was after Amanda's trouble that I got my life on track. In a way, I had Amanda to thank.

"Fast forward. Marc bought and renamed your company and kept you on as an advisor. You're here to represent the collection. You told Marc about Nick, and now he's here too."

"I just thought Nick should hear Marc out. Nick has options that I didn't. He double majored in design and business, and he worked for a bunch of companies before he went out on his own. He could make five phone calls and have a job by the end of the month."

"But he didn't. For all I know, while I'm here working the Intimate Mode show"—I ignored Amanda's raised eyebrow at the word "working"—"Marc is trying to set up Nick as the creative director of one of his companies."

I glanced at the clock. It was long past visiting hours at the hospital. I didn't doubt they'd bend the rules for someone of Marc's financial background—heck, I didn't even doubt he'd make a generous donation to them on the spot to gain favor. I'd do the same thing if I had his money and Nick was the one in the hospital. No judgment.

But the longer the two of them were gone, the more concerned I became that they were bonding like Amanda and I were. Would Marc offer Nick a job? Would Nick take it? If so, how would that affect Nick's and my future?

———

As the night wore on and the champagne bottles emptied, it seemed inevitable that Amanda's and my night would turn into a slumber party. Amanda curled up on the sofa, and I draped a blanket over her.

"Go to sleep. I'll set the alarm so you can get to your hotel in the morning before the Intimate Mode show."

"Okay," she said, her voice sounding halfway to dreamland. As I reached the door, she spoke. "Samantha."

"Yes?"

"I never said thank you."

I smiled, though in the dark she probably couldn't see. "You didn't have to." I picked up a keycard and left.

———

I had questions. Too many questions to sleep. I wanted to talk them out, but there wasn't anybody around who could help me. I wandered into the casino, hoping to find a distraction. I weaved through the slot machines, barely registering the colors and sounds. Before I knew it, I was out of the casino and headed toward the chapel. I had no idea why.

Yes, I did.

I was troubled, and there was something about the quiet, peaceful zone behind those doors that offered calm. And also, I wanted to find out more about that guestbook.

Tonight, Irene was wearing a light-blue straw pillbox hat with netting by her forehead. Her floral dress and short jacket held tones of blue, purple, and green, and her lips were an iridescent shade of coral. She smiled, revealing a transfer of lipstick onto her two front teeth. Involuntarily, I ran my tongue over my front teeth to make sure I didn't reflect her makeup fail.

"Well, hello there!" she greeted me. "You were here a few nights ago. Has your fella gotten over his nerves yet?"

"Pretty much," I said.

"I shouldn't tell you this, but he came back after the two of you left and said you're the one who's nervous about getting married. Isn't that sweet? He wanted to give you some alone time to talk to Chaplain Rick so you felt comfortable before making any decisions. If you ask me, too many people rush into marriage before they're ready. It's nice to see you two taking this seriously."

I knew Nick had come back to the chapel to return the guestbook, but I hadn't known he'd used our circumstances as his cover. It touched me that Nick had confided in Irene and that he'd shared his concerns that I wasn't ready to commit.

"Is that why you're here? To seek counsel?" she asked.

"Actually, I wanted to sneak a peek at the guestbook." I didn't know if my request was normal or not, so I added, "It's comforting to see all those people who are so sure about their decision."

"Sure, honey. I was just working on it."

"Working on it how? I would think people sign in and that's it."

"Yes, except the other night I spilled my coffee on it, and two of the pages stuck together. I tore them out, but it's a shame not to have a record of those weddings in here. I told Chaplain Rick I'd copy them all in myself." She opened the book and pulled out two soiled pages. "I'm sure nobody cares about this but me, but it just seems like the right thing to do."

"May I?" I asked, reaching for the pages.

She handed them to me, and I scanned the entries. The pages were wrinkled in the way of wet paper that's dried. And three-quarters of the way down on the second page was an almost illegible entry: Marc Rico and Chryssinda Sykes.

It seemed the missing pages in the guestbook were a dead end. At least it seemed that way until I spotted the name of the witness for the nuptials: Joey Cheeks.

31

A LIGHTWEIGHT

"THIS NAME, JOEY CHEEKS—DO YOU REMEMBER HIM?" I asked.

"We all know Joey. He's a regular around here," Irene answered.

"Do you mean he likes to gamble?" I lowered my voice. "Does he have a problem?"

She laughed. "Oh, no, dear. He's married to our hotel manager."

"Alain Remie?" I said. "Alain is married to Joey?"

"Yes, such sweet boys. Joey used to work here as an Elvis impersonator to get money to finance his collection. That's how they met."

This meant something, I knew it. Alain had taken the photo of Lydia that ended up in the newspapers. The photo that showed off Joey's brand slogan across her bottom. The photo was in such poor taste that I'd assumed Alain was an opportunistic parasite who'd probably been selling off images like that for years, but this took it to another level. When Alain took that photo, he knew he'd be using Lydia's death to further his husband's career trajectory.

Either Marbury was doing a poor job investigating, or he knew all this and hadn't told me. I hated when the police played their cards close to their chest.

"Dear, you look a little pale. Can I get you a bottle of water?"

"No, thank you. I'm just feeling a little lightheaded."

She patted my hand. "Don't try to rush things. You'll know when the time is right."

I left the chapel and tried to call Nick again. This time the call went directly to voicemail. Either his phone was off, or his battery had died. It was well past midnight, and the aftereffects of the champagne and too much mental energy spent trying to figure out what was going on left me exhausted. I went back to the room and found Amanda asleep in my bed.

I took a quick shower and changed into pajamas. As silly as it seemed, I felt responsible for Amanda. I scribbled a note to Nick and left it on the door, grabbed a spare blanket, and slept on the sofa.

———

THE NEXT MORNING came all too quickly. It wasn't my alarm that woke me. It was Amanda. "Samantha," she said, gently shaking me. "Wake up."

"Huh?"

"How much did we drink last night?"

I blinked against the bright light streaming into the room and slowly picked out several empty champagne bottles. "That wasn't us. That was Kristin and Sue Ellen. We mostly stuck to splits from the minibar."

"Then explain this hangover." She had her hands on her head.

I shook myself awake and sat up. "I don't know. You're a lightweight?" I squinted at the clock. "It's only six-thirty. Why are you awake?"

"It's the last day of the trade show. I'm double booked with appointments. I have to get to my hotel, get ready, and get to Flush before the shows open."

"I'll meet you there."

I removed the Privacy sign from the door in the hopes maid service would arrive early and went to Marc's room, expecting to find the men crashed in much the same manner (without empty champagne bottles) as Amanda and me.

Nobody answered my knock.

I admit I started to worry. Had the people who threatened Marc gotten to them while they were out? Or had Nick being a friend to Marc turned into another guys' night out?

I called the hospital and asked for an update on Chryssinda's condition. The woman refused to tell me anything, saying the information was protected by HIPAA guidelines. I asked if two men had come to visit her. She politely explained that answering that question would confirm Chryssinda's hospital presence. Finally, out of desperation, I cut to the chase.

"I'm trying to reach my fiancé. He isn't answering his phone."

"Well, dear, we do have a strict no cell phone policy, so hypothetically speaking, if he had come here, he would likely have turned his phone off or set it to silent."

"'Hypothetically speaking?'"

"That's the best I can do."

"Sure, that makes sense." I thanked the nurse and hung up, mildly impressed with her ability to both protect and skirt the rules.

Amanda, being an employee of one of Marc's companies, would have his phone number. When I arrived at Intimate Mode, I'd have her call him to make sure they were okay.

For my last day at the lingerie fair, I dressed in an oversized white shirt which I belted loosely at my waist, narrow black pants, and black ballerina flats. I tied a pink scarf around my neck and spun the knot to the side. I caught the Deuce and arrived at Flush just as the doors were opening. The last day of a trade show is usually the busiest since many vendors relax their security measures to meet new contacts and give away swag they don't care to pack up. I was headed directly for Amanda's booth when I heard my name.

"Samantha Kidd from Tradava! Wait up!"

Even before I turned around, I knew who it was.

Slowly I pivoted and watched as Joey Cheeks approached. Anxiety filled me, but his expression looked even more fearful than I felt.

"Joey," I said. "Good morning."

"It's not all that good for me. I spent the night in the police station. Somebody told them I murdered Lydia and knocked out Chryssinda. Do you know anything about that?"

"I don't think this is the appropriate place to have this conversation," I said.

"Come to my booth," he said. "We canceled all of our appointments. I need to explain to you what happened."

That got my attention. I followed him to the Blue section, behind the pink velvet stanchion, into the back room. Teresa, sporting a T-shirt that said #OverIt, black nylon track pants with white stripes down the side, and highlighter-yellow patent leather stilettos, remained in front of the curtain by a table filled with tiny gift bags. She handed them out freely to anyone within a five-foot radius of the booth.

"What happened to protecting the secrecy of your designs?" I asked Joey.

"I don't care anymore. I want anything with the #GetCheeky logo on it out of my sight."

"Why? Three days ago, you were ready to be the star of this whole show."

"You accused me of murder. You accused my husband of selling a publicity photo for financial gain. If his hotel believed those accusations, he'd lose his entire career. Neither one of us would work in this town again."

"Didn't he?" I asked.

"Didn't he what?"

"Sell a tasteless publicity photo of Lydia's dead body to the *Las Vegas Sun* for financial gain?"

Joey looked horrified. "No!" He looked away, chewed his bottom lip, and took off his Elvis glasses. Without them, he looked young and innocent. "You believe everything you told the police, don't you?"

"I wouldn't tell them lies," I said.

"I had a photo shoot at The Left Bank. Lydia was in the Marry Rich: Pending T-shirt and the #GetCheeky panties. I booked a whole group of models for a mock bachelorette party, tacky veil and all."

"I saw them in the lobby."

"That's my exact point. The pictures Alain took were of the photo shoot. I told Lydia I wanted some natural, un-posed shots. Like outtakes. I wanted something I could use on social media to make the entire campaign seem like fun."

"More reality show than advertising campaign."

"Exactly. The photo that ended up in the newspapers was taken while Lydia was alive. I never would have used it if I'd known she was murdered. The story we leaked was 'lingerie photo shoot at The Left Bank kicks off Intimate Mode fashion show.' Alain thought it was a good way to get publicity for his hotel plus a little boost for Cheeky

Panties. The paper paid him a standard two-hundred-dollar fee for the copyright. The *Las Vegas Sun* made all the money selling that photo to other papers, not him."

"What about Teresa? What did she think of it?"

"What does Teresa have to do with it?"

"I saw you two argue during Yarvi Tatum's presentation. What was that about?"

"You don't miss a trick, do you?" He shook his head. "Teresa gave her notice two weeks ago. She shouldn't even be here. But I needed help, and somebody had to run interference between me and Lydia. I begged Teresa to keep it quiet—promised her a five-thousand-dollar bonus too—and she agreed. But the house that panties built is collapsing." He smoothed the sides of his gelled hair with his palms. "Teresa wants her money, and she wants out."

The words had a ring of familiarity to them. They were almost verbatim what I'd heard his line manager say when I was hiding under the stage.

I looked away from Joey and thought through what he said. I first took note of Lydia in the lobby while checking in. She, and all of the women, were dressed in their Marry Rich T-shirts, and Chryssinda had been hot-gluing condoms to Lydia's veil. Lydia had been on the phone, and she'd been annoyed.

"You and Lydia fought about something that day," I said.

"Lydia was a diva. I'd just found out some sleazy

tabloid was saying she used to work in the escort industry. That's not the image I hired her for."

"Marry Rich T-shirts?"

"It was too coincidental. If I put a bunch of models in those T-shirts, it would have been funny. But when a story breaks that one of those models worked as a high-class call girl, my brand goes in the toilet."

"That looks a lot like motive. Plus you said you wanted to find a way out of Lydia's contract. Murder is one way out."

He looked shocked. "How do you know about that conversation?"

It was not the time to lie. "I overheard you telling Teresa. And then I heard Chryssinda tell Teresa she thought you were involved in Lydia's death."

Joey paled. "And Chryssinda's body was found in my booth. No wonder you thought I was involved."

I studied him. The Elvis bravado was gone. It was like a vacuum had sucked the confidence and high energy out of him, leaving a scared little boy who didn't know which way to turn. My heart went out to him, but my head wasn't 100% on board with his story. Not yet.

"Joey, I saw you the day I arrived in Las Vegas. You and Chryssinda were on the sidewalk between The Left Bank and Paris. You looked like—well, you looked like you always do, but Chryssinda was dressed like Madonna. You were in the same spot where Lydia's body was found. It looked to me like you were casing the background. Maybe for later?"

Joey looked like I'd given him a suitcase filled with cash. His eyes got bright, and he leaned forward. "You're right. Did you tell the police?"

"I didn't figure that out until last night, but I plan to show them the pictures today." Why was he so happy? I'd expected him to be sweating bullets right now.

"You took our picture?"

"Yes. Why?"

He leaned forward and kissed me on the cheek. "Thank you, Samantha Kidd from Tradava!"

"Thank me for what?"

"You're the proof I need. I left the shoot early to work a private celebrity wedding party. I performed two sets as Elvis at their pre-reception and accompanied them to the airport for their honeymoon in Hawaii. I told the police, but they can't verify my alibi because the couple is unreachable, and I don't get my copy of the confidentiality contract until they return."

"Surely somebody else could back you up?"

He leaned forward. "Elvis impersonators are a dime a dozen around here. But if you took pictures, those pictures show me in costume. They fit my timeline. That would be enough to make the police track down the celebrities to confirm my statement. They'll see there was no way I could have been involved."

32

ILLUSION

WHATEVER VACUUM HAD SUCKED THE LIFE OUT OF JOEY shifted to me. He couldn't have murdered Lydia, not if he was in a private ceremony with people who could afford private planes, Elvis impersonators, and confidential nondisclosure agreements. Joey couldn't be in two places at the same time, and the evidence showed me that on the night in question, Elvis had left the building. Beyond a shadow of a doubt.

I apologized for the trouble I'd caused and promised to write an order for Tradava when I returned home. Joey seemed genuinely happy with the apology and not particularly concerned with the order, which told me Joey had a new respect for the priorities of life. I left his booth and wandered back into the trade show.

The answer to the puzzle had to be here somewhere. Both Lydia and Chryssinda were lingerie models. Their day jobs brought them to Intimate Mode. Lydia had been found dead in the very product line she was contracted to represent, and Chryssinda's body had been left behind in the designer's booth. Someone was using Joey's love of the limelight to create the illusion that he was a murderer.

Holy smokes. *Illusion.* That was the key to everything. The information I gave the police, the trail of clues I'd followed, the trickle of information that had forced Flush Casino to double down on security measures and screen every attendee at the trade show. It all was for one reason.

To throw us off the scent of the real murderer.

———

ON MY WAY to Amanda's booth, I bumped into Lisa, the buxom black model who had coached me through my bang-bang reveal on Yarvi's runway presentation.

"Girl, slow down! You wanna run, you better put on a sports bra."

"I can't slow down."

"Then hold your girls in place. Otherwise, they're going to be down by your knees before you hit forty." She grabbed my wrists and placed my hands on my boobs. "Go."

I rounded the corner and waved my hands to get Amanda's attention. She was assessing a rack of samples and a trio of models, two that I recognized as Kristin and

Sue Ellen from last night. I grabbed three hangers from the rolling rack and dealt them to the women. "Make it work," I said. "I have to talk to Amanda."

Sue Ellen handed the red robe to Kristin and took the aqua robe from the third woman. They looked at Amanda, who said, "Fine," and pointed to the changing screen.

I grabbed Amanda's forearm and pulled her to a secluded corner. "Have you heard from Nick and Marc?"

"Not today. Why?"

I waved my hand back and forth. "No time to explain. Do you have Marc's number? Nick's phone is either off or dead, and I need to reach them."

"Sure."

She scrolled through her contacts until she found the number. She read it off, and I typed it into my phone.

"Thanks. I have to go."

"Samantha!" she called out. "What can I do?"

"Keep an eye on Teresa Kander."

"Teresa? Joey's line manager?" Amanda's features scrunched together in confusion. "What does she have to do with anything?"

I was fairly sure Teresa had nothing to do with anything. If Amanda kept her eyes on Teresa, then Amanda would be nowhere near the murderer. "I'll explain everything later. Trust me."

I collected my things and left the show. On my way back to The Left Bank, I called Marc.

"Marc Rico," he answered.

"Marc, it's Samantha Kidd."

"Sammie, what's up?"

"Is Nick with you?"

"He's in the john. Why?"

"I haven't been able to reach him since the two of you left last night. Is everything okay? With Chryssinda?"

"Chryssie is going to be fine," he said. There was a note of blind optimism in his voice, and I wondered if he believed the power of positive thinking was going to pull her out of her coma, or if he knew something I didn't (which could pretty much be anything considering the HIPAA guidelines).

"Are you at Intimate Mode?" he asked.

"I just left. I'm headed back to The Left Bank."

"Done already?"

"Yes. To be honest, I don't think the lingerie business is right for me. With the attack on Chryssinda and some things I've found out about one of the vendors here, I don't feel all that comfortable."

"Do you know who is responsible?"

"I have a suspicion, and that's enough. I can't shake the fact that somebody here has been watching me. If staying away from Intimate Mode can keep those people safe, then I'll stay away."

"Nick's a lucky guy," Marc said. "It's too bad you got caught up in this."

"With any luck, it'll all be over soon."

The Deuce pulled up in front of The Bellagio, and I exited. It was a short walk to The Left Bank, and when

I entered the hotel, I went straight to the concierge desk. Jacques was working, and he froze when he saw me.

"Miss Kidd," he said, with no trace of an accent.

"*Bonjour*, Jacques," I said. "*Comment allez-vous*?" It was one of the few French phrases I remembered from high school, and I hoped that by speaking his adopted language, I could show him I was making an effort to respect his cover.

He didn't reply.

"*Je suis* Samantha Kidd," I said. "*Mon crayon est grand et jaune.*"

"Your pencil is big and yellow?" he asked.

"It's a line from *Gotcha*. I'm running out of French."

"I see." He looked to his left and right and back to me. "Eees there anything I can help you weeeth, Meees Keeed?"

I smiled. "In fact, there is. Have you seen Nick Taylor or Marc Rico today?"

"*Oui.* Ze two men are upstairs. They called for room service not long ago."

"Perfect. Have there been any unusual charges on their room service bill?"

"*Non.*"

"Perfect again. Would you relay a message to Nick for me? Tell him I'm going to pick out my dress and veil in the wedding store in the lobby and will be coming to the room to get changed in half an hour. It's bad luck for the groom to see the bride before the ceremony, so I prefer if he's not there. He knows I'm superstitious. He'll understand."

Jacques looked surprised. "You're getting married here? At The Left Bank?"

I shrugged. "It seems almost too convenient, right? Especially with his friend Marc here. I couldn't ask for a better opportunity. I can trust you to tell him, right?"

"But of course."

"One more thing," I said. I reached over the counter and picked up a notepad and a pen. "I have one friend in Las Vegas who I'd like present. Detective Marbury. Can you call him at this number and ask him to come to The Left Bank as soon as possible?"

"Sure," Jacques said. By this point, his accent was dropping in and out, and I doubted he even knew it.

I left Jacques in stunned disbelief and went to the bridal salon. Assuming he'd call Marc's room, I knew I'd be expected upstairs in half an hour. That was half an hour to kill shopping for overpriced bridal attire for a wedding that wasn't going to take place.

I bought a veil, browsed the clearance dresses, and went to my room. It was neat and tidy. The maid service had removed all signs of the mess Kristin, Sue Ellen, Amanda, and I had left behind. I poked my head out the door and looked down the hall. The room service cart I'd pushed into the hallway was gone.

I rooted through my suitcase for one particular sample from Intimate Mode. It was a small gift bag from Joey Cheeks, and inside was a T-shirt that said

#RealityIsOverrated. I took off my white shirt and pulled on the tee, changed out of my cropped black pants and into a pair of #GetCheeky panties, and brushed out my hair until it was full and bouncy. I slipped the white veil on and looked at my reflection. Was I going to do this?

Yes. I was. Because nobody else could do it for me, and if I didn't do it, nobody could end the cycle.

33

GAMBLING

I left my room and went to Marc Rico's suite. The Do Not Disturb sign hung on the door. I knocked, and Marc opened the door seconds later.

"Sammie," he said. His eyes moved from the top of my head, down my torso to my feet, and back to my face. "This is a surprise. Come on in." He held the door open, and I entered. Unlike my newly serviced room, his bedsheets were tossed, and empty bottles of booze lined the windowsill.

"Is Nick here?" I asked.

He hesitated. "No. He's downstairs in the casino."

Jacques had told me Nick was up here, and I'd been counting on that as part of my plan. I'd also counted on Jacques getting Detective Marbury to the hotel. What if I'd made a mistake relying on Jacques?

"You're a bad influence." I joked. "What's Nick's game today?"

"The usual. You know Nick."

"Not when it comes to Vegas. We've barely set foot in the casino. You probably know more about his gambling habits than I do."

Marc studied me. "Blackjack."

"Blackjack?" I repeated.

"Does that surprise you?" He snapped his fingers. "Quick decisions. Calculate your odds. Fast money. It's a risk taker's game."

But Nick wasn't into blackjack for the very reasons Marc claimed to like the game. And if Marc had paid attention while he was at the casino with Nick, he'd know that.

Was Nick in the casino or was he somewhere else?

"I left a message for Nick at the front desk, so I should probably check in with Jacques to see if he was able to reach him." I headed toward the door.

"It would be bad luck for him to see you," Marc said. "Use my phone."

"That's okay. Nick's probably either waiting for me in our room or outside the chapel."

"What's the rush? Come here. Let me adjust your veil."

I felt the walls closing in on me. I'd asked Jacques to deliver not one but two messages. How long until Marbury was here? Twenty minutes? Thirty? I had to wait out the moment and act like everything was fine.

I crossed the room and faced the full-length mirror. Marc stood behind me and fluffed my veil. "You look just like she did before she died," he whispered in my ear. "Did you think I wouldn't notice?"

My blood ran cold, and I stiffened.

"Relax, Sammie. There's no point in worrying about things you can't control. But I should tell you Nick's not waiting in your room or outside the chapel," Marc said. He locked eyes with my reflection, and my skin felt prickly. "He's not playing blackjack. He didn't get your message, and he's not going to join us."

I didn't know if Marc was lying or telling the truth. I didn't know if Detective Marbury was on his way or if that message hadn't been delivered either. The only thing I knew was if I didn't get out of the room, I'd end up a victim.

"I know it was you," I said softly. "You knew exactly how the police would investigate what appeared to be a suicide because you lived through the investigation with Pamela Martin."

Marc's hands stopped adjusting the fabric of the veil. I looked into the mirror and caught his eyes.

"You don't know anything," he said.

"You tried to make it look like Lydia killed herself. If her death were ruled a suicide, you'd be in the clear. You even tried to feed Nick info—fake memories of you two hanging out together while Lydia supposedly jumped to her death. You thought you could use Amanda too."

"I thought my money would buy more than her pathetic company."

"All of the clues pointed to something at Intimate

Mode. But there wasn't anybody at Intimate Mode who wanted Lydia or Chryssinda dead. There was absolutely nothing at the entire show that held any sort of a threat to either one of them."

"That's quite an imagination you've got, Samantha."

For all the times I'd wanted to hear him say my actual name, the sound of him speaking it now chilled me to my bones. "There weren't any death threats against you, were there? Nobody is claiming to come after you for what happened to Pamela. You made that all up to insulate yourself. That's why there were no calls to ping off cell phone towers. You made it all up. You are cold and calculated and evil and greedy. There was no security detail watching over Lydia when you and Nick made a scene at The Heart Club. You did that to create an alibi. You murdered Lydia Moss and attempted to murder Chryssinda."

Marc Rico's eyes were flat and emotionless. Creases by the sides of his mouth deepened. His face looked as though it had been carved from a rock. Deep circles under his dark-brown eyes aged him. Yesterday, those circles had given him the appearance of an exhausted new groom who was worried about his wife's safety. Today, the safest thing for Chryssinda was for me to keep Marc away from her.

"I knew you were going to be a problem," he said. His hands hovered over the veil, and I sensed his body tense. If he wanted to, he could have strangled me right then and there.

"That's right. You didn't count on me, did you? You hired Amanda to work for you at Intimate Mode. She'd be the perfect eyes and ears." I thought about what Amanda had told me. "It must have been like a gift from the universe when she called you for a job."

"I haven't thought about those days at I-FAD for a very long time. Amanda brought it all back. Chryssinda should have left things the way they were. But her friend Lydia had a big mouth and knew too much about my business. She told Chryssie I was the big payoff. Two working girls thought they could trap me into marriage and get half my money."

"You said Chryssinda had her own money."

"Chryssinda's 'family money' came from me. I wired five million into an account to make her look respectable. If people knew she was after my money, they'd know I had a reason to kill her."

"But if you wanted her dead, then why did you marry her?"

"She caught me killing Lydia. I had to keep her quiet. Forcing her to marry me was my insurance policy. Keep her close. I could have killed her whenever I wanted. She knew that. I had complete control over her."

He was talking too much. Telling me things that could send him to jail. We both knew why. Marc didn't expect me to leave the room alive.

"And Nick? Why did you get him involved?" I asked.

"Nick should've been so drunk he passed out in my room. When he left in search of you, I had to find a way to account for my time. I threatened Chryssinda's life, and she played her new role perfectly. And a wife can't testify against her husband. It was the perfect insurance."

Extorting money from Marc had been Lydia's idea. That had bothered me, how a lingerie model who was nothing more than a friend of a businessman's fiancée would know intimate details of his financial life: how often he was hit up for money and how much he could afford to lose. This plan of hers and Chryssinda's explained why she cared so much about people asking for Marc's money. Everything I'd seen that first night, the diva attitude, the protectiveness over her man, the dismissive attitude of Nick and me, it was all her protecting what she and Chryssinda had set into play.

I turned around and faced Marc. The mirror was behind me. We were less than a foot apart. I was nervous, more nervous than I'd ever been in my life, but I couldn't let Marc see fear.

"You used Nick as your alibi. Spontaneous bachelor party with your old college friend. Clever. You got Nick so drunk he didn't remember what happened—you tested his memory in our room. You killed Lydia, and when Chryssinda caught you, you forced her to the chapel for an unexpected ceremony—paying off another couple for their spot. All part of the plan, right? Throw money around, show the world you can't wait to marry your bride, so when her best friend is found dead the next day, you can make people think Lydia killed herself. You were going to make it look like she was secretly in love with you."

"Is that what you think?"

"I think you lined up multiple witnesses who can verify your whereabouts the night Lydia died."

"Not to mention the chapel guestbook," Marc said with a smile.

"See, that's the thing," I said. I looked past him and tapped my finger against my lips as if thinking about what I already knew. "Irene, the lady at the wedding chapel, spilled a cup of coffee on the guestbook, and the pages got ruined. She tore them out so the rest of the book wouldn't be soiled, and now she's recopying the names. When Detective Marbury follows up on that, your signature isn't going to be in there, is it? Shame."

Marc's eyes narrowed. "You expect me to believe that?"

"And then there's Joey Cheeks, who you tried to set up. But Joey is married to the hotel manager, Alain Remie. The photo of Lydia in the newspapers was taken while Lydia was alive. During a photo shoot that was prearranged. Alain already turned his pictures and camera over to the police to verify what time the picture was taken."

"That doesn't tell anybody anything."

"No, I guess it doesn't." I took a deep breath as if giving up. "Well, it wouldn't tell anybody anything if Nick hadn't set his iPad up to take a time-lapse video of the sun going down over the Eiffel Tower on our very first day here. You know, we changed rooms so many times that we stopped unpacking. That iPad is just sitting in the bottom of my suitcase. Now, I wonder, when the police analyze it frame by frame, will they see anything unusual? I know Lydia didn't jump like the placement of her body suggested. You put her there."

If this were a game of poker, then I'd just bet the house on a bogus hand. There was no time-lapse video. Nick and I had changed rooms so many times the first day we were here that he'd abandoned the idea. There was nothing incriminating to show Marc Rico depositing Lydia Moss's body in the common area outside The Left Bank, but Marc didn't know that.

If Marc Rico discovered I was bluffing before help arrived, one thing was certain: Nick would be left standing at the altar.

34

BLUFFING

I watched Marc closely. I didn't doubt he had the mental acuity to make strategic business decisions, gamble on investments, and predict the competition's next move before they knew they were being watched. And had Marc spent any amount of time around me since we'd first met, he might have had a chance. But he hadn't. He'd bet everything on Nick and Amanda, loyalties and long-buried emotions from college days. And now that they both appeared to need something from him, he thought he could exploit their dependency to let him get away with murder. He hadn't known Nick never got over his suspicions, and he hadn't known Nick would confide in me.

No, Marc Rico had never seen me coming.

"You're bluffing," he said. "If you had any evidence, you would have turned it over to the police."

"Well, see, that's one of my flaws. I tend to think I can

figure things out that the police can't. Surely you learned about that from Nick, right? There's this cop in Pennsylvania, Detective Loncar, and he'd probably arrest me if he could come up with charges that stuck. Even Nick and I broke up over it once. One of these days, I'll learn my lesson, I'm sure."

Marc reached up under the veil and grabbed my hair. He yanked my head backward, and the sudden moment caused a stab of pain to shoot through my neck. He put his lips up against my ear. "Show me the iPad," he hissed.

I didn't have to act to make tears appear. I twisted my neck to minimize the pain. Marc jerked my head the other direction. My shoulders hunched. I blinked several times to free the tears. It didn't matter how well I acted to try to trick him. Pain was pain.

Marc turned me toward the door and pushed. There was no point dragging my feet or digging in my heels. Nobody was going to come crashing through the doors of Marc Rico's room to save me. This man had rented out the entire floor. The room service bill I'd racked up in the past three days was probably higher than my monthly mortgage payment, and it was built on twenty-two variations of mac and cheese and champagne for hookers. Marc's mini-fridge was stocked with more groceries than I bought in a month.

I'd come up against greedy people, desperate people, jilted people, and corrupt people. I'd never taken on someone who saw people as commodities that could be traded like futures on orange juice. I had zero sense of the level of power money could give a person like Marc Rico, but with his fist twisted up in my hair underneath a cheap veil I'd bought in a Las Vegas boutique, I knew if we went head to head, he'd win.

Winning for him meant getting away with murder.

Losing for me meant dying.

It wasn't a gamble I was willing to take.

We were halfway to the door when I remembered what Sandra Bullock had taught me in the *Miss Congeniality* movies. It was time to SING.

I balled up my fist and drove my elbow backward into Marc's solar plexus. He doubled over and yelled. Before he could recover, I stomped onto his instep. He let go of my head, and I slammed it backward. His scream confirmed that I connected with his nose. I whirled around and kneed him in the groin.

Marc dropped to the floor. He grabbed my ankle.

I tried to kick him off. He was too strong. He pulled my leg toward him with one hand and in the other held a syringe.

Where'd he get a syringe?

An image of Chryssinda's closed eyes and limp body flashed into my mind. Was this what he'd used to put Chryssinda in the coma that put her in the hospital? And how he kept her in that coma after his visit last night?

With a renewed desire to flee, I jerked my foot back and forth. My shoe came loose. I bent down to grab it. The veil fell off my head and landed on Marc. He cursed. His grip relaxed. I jerked my foot away and ran to the door. It took two attempts to get it open. I ran to the elevators. My ankle felt hot like I'd been stung by a bee. As I stumbled down the hall and felt my extremities go numb, I glanced down and confirmed the worst thing I could have imagined.

Marc had injected me before I'd gotten out of the room. The syringe was hanging from my ankle.

35

NOT A PROUD MOMENT

Nick found me in the hallway. Face down. In my #RealityIsOverrated T-shirt and #GetCheeky panties. One shoe on, one shoe off and a broken needle jutting out of my flesh. My veil was on the floor ten feet behind me.

It was not a proud moment, but I was alive.

Detective Marbury found Marc Rico on the staircase between the sixth and seventh floor. A helicopter was circling the building. Had he gotten to the roof, odds were he could have disappeared in a way that would have required extradition to prosecute him.

The odds weren't in his favor.

Yay.

Between what I could tell him and what he was able to discover after searching Marc's room, Detective Marbury pieced together what had happened: Marc Rico had murdered Lydia Moss and attempted murder on

Chryssinda Sykes and me. He used high doses of an injectable skeletal muscle relaxer to incapacitate each of us. In Lydia's case, he gave her an overdose of painkillers while she couldn't fight back. The pain meds would be detectable on a standard toxicology screening, confirming suspicions of suicide, but the muscle relaxer wouldn't.

Marc's whole plan had been to tie the models to a scandal at the lingerie fair and let the industry implode under the pressure of perfection heaped on top of models. His guidebook had been the death of Pamela Martin twenty years before. He had a front-row seat to the police investigation and knew which questions would be asked, which tests would be run, and which alibis would stand. He also knew which drugs would get the job done, and he knew how to get them.

Deep pockets weren't just a fashion statement.

———

My return flight to Ribbon was scheduled for Thursday. Neither Nick nor I were on it. With Marc no longer paying for our room, when the hospital released me, we had no place to go.

"How did you figure it out?" Nick asked.

I sat in a wheelchair—hospital insurance policy dictated I remain in one until I was off their property— and he sat in a chair next to me. He had my left hand sandwiched between both of his.

"I kept thinking about the clues. Every single clue pointed to the lingerie fair. But I was at the lingerie fair, and nobody acted like they thought anything bad had happened. I kept wondering why nobody was scared, and it finally occurred to me that it was because the crimes had nothing to do with them. To all the vendors inside Intimate Mode, it was business as usual."

Except Chryssinda. She'd been the one to stash the cone bra in my #GetCheeky swag bag. Not because she wanted me to have it, but because she had to get it out of Joey's booth.

"What about the hotel? The guestbook from the chapel?"

"I talked to Irene. She told me she spilled coffee on the guestbook and tore out the pages so they wouldn't stain the other entries. Your solicitation charge—"

"Suspicion of solicitation," Nick corrected.

I rolled my eyes. "Brought Kristin and Sue Ellen to our room, except they thought it was Marc's room because our room was on his bill. But why would Marc hire escorts if he was upset about his wife? That's how I found out about Jacques and his side business."

"The Left Bank concierge runs the escort service?"

"Yes. And I'm sure if Alain Remie learned the truth, Jacques would be out of a job."

"Are you going to tell him?"

"No." I squeezed Nick's hand. "Once Jacques knew I knew about his side business, he became very cooperative. If he hadn't called the police like I asked, I'd be—not here."

I wasn't the only one who had suspicions about Marc. Nick had too. He just hadn't expected me to force Marc's hand with my spontaneous wedding ceremony act and had been sitting vigil by Chryssinda's side to make sure Marc couldn't get to her. The only problem with his plan was that Marc had lied to him about my whereabouts, giving him a constant stream of updates about my shenanigans at Intimate Mode. It was Amanda who finally reached Nick and told him I was in trouble. Not because she suspected the truth, but because she knew if anything happened to me, Nick might not recover.

That's the funny thing about friendship. Once you realize who the people are that you want in your life, you do what you have to do to protect them. Sometimes those people let you in, and sometimes they don't. I'd spent years operating as a free agent, and I was done. It was time for the next chapter. I didn't want to die alone in a Las Vegas hallway wearing nothing but a T-shirt, panties, and a tacky wedding veil.

Hypothetically speaking, of course.

EPILOGUE

Alain Remie comped our room at The Left Bank for the duration of our time in Vegas. It took two days for the physical effects of the injection and the fight with Marc to fade. I briefly wondered if the Associated Press would mention me in the news surrounding Marc Rico's downfall. The question was answered when the flowers started arriving: from friends, family, and even my old friend Detective Loncar.

I milked my recuperation time and sampled all twenty-two versions of mac and cheese from the comfort of my king-sized bed. While I recovered, Nick acted as my unofficial assistant, faxing my lingerie orders to Tradava and arranging a few extra days of unpaid leave. It was three days later when Nick returned to the room to find me sitting on the corner of the bed.

"It's time for something different," I said.

"I didn't think you were ever going to get tired of mac and cheese."

"I'm not talking about mac and cheese." In my hand was the $50 poker chip Jacques had given me when Nick and I first checked in. "Wanna gamble?"

"On what?"

"You know what."

Nick nodded. I opened my hand and showed him the chip. "You said when you gamble, you want the universe to determine the outcome. No thought involved. We could bet it all on roulette."

"That requires us to pick a number."

"Well, I've been thinking about that." I took his hand. "You know that scene in *Casablanca* when the lady who goes to Rick for money plays roulette and keeps winning on twenty-two?"

"Yes, but isn't that also the number Julie Hagerty keeps betting on in *Lost in America*? The reason she loses her and Albert Brooks' nest egg?"

"Yes. The way I see it, those two movies cancel each other out."

He sat down next to me. "If only there were a sign that said the number twenty-two was significant."

"Like the number of mac and cheese selections on the menu?"

He smiled. "Works for me."

THE UNIVERSE WAS FEELING ROMANTIC. Chaplain Rick conducted the ceremony, and Irene wore a pink floral shift dress and matching flowerpot hat for the occasion. Nick asked Amanda to be his witness, and I Skyped Eddie (and Logan) in via my laptop to act as mine. The Left Bank tossed in both Elvis and Ann-Margret at no additional charge.

We honeymooned in Paris. The real one. And the Eiffel Tower was every bit as spectacular as I'd hoped.

FROM DIANE

Hi! Did you see that coming? That epilogue? You *did* read that far, didn't you? That wasn't how I thought this book was going to end, but there was a time when I didn't even know if this book was going to *have* an ending, mostly because Samantha was being difficult. But we worked things out.

When I originally conceived of this book, it was going to be set in Paris. I have half of that book in a file somewhere—but Samantha didn't like it. At the suggestion of a friend, I set down the computer and had a conversation with her. (Samantha, not the friend.) (Yes. I had a conversation with a fictional character. You're not all that surprised, are you?

She hit me with her concerns about the original book, and they were valid. We struck a deal. I gave her two days to tell me a new story. If she did, I'd write it. If she didn't, I'd go back to the original file with the choppy draft that she didn't like. Guess which one happened? She told me enough in those first two days to send me off to Las Vegas —not Paris—and find out even more about Nick's backstory than we learned in the previous book.

And as a thank you to her for cooperating, I let her go to Paris after all.

Xo,

Diane

ABOUT THE AUTHOR

National bestselling author Diane Vallere writes smart, funny, and fashionable character-based mysteries. After two decades working for a top luxury retailer, she traded fashion accessories for accessories to murder. A past president of Sisters in Crime, Diane started her own detective agency at age ten and has maintained a passion for shoes, clues, and clothes ever since. Find out more at dianevallere.com.

ACKNOWLEDGMENTS

Special thanks to: Jenette Goldstein from Jenette Bras for taking the time to chat about the lingerie business, Teresa Kander for allowing use of her name, Gretchen Archer for suggesting I ask Samantha what she didn't like about my original idea, The Polyester Posse, for helping my books gain visibility, Ramona deFelice Long for editorial guidance, the members of Shoptalk, The Atelier, and the subscribers of The Weekly DiVa, who brighten my world.

ALSO BY

<u>Samantha Kidd Mysteries</u>

Designer Dirty Laundry

Buyer, Beware

The Brim Reaper

Some Like It Haute

Grand Theft Retro

Pearls Gone Wild

Cement Stilettos

Panty Raid

Union Jacked

Slay Ride

Tough Luxe

Fahrenheit 501

Stark Raving Mod

Gilt Trip

Ranch Dressing

<u>Madison Night Mad for Mod Mysteries</u>

"Midnight Ice" (prequel novella)

Pillow StalkThat Touch of Ink

With Vics You Get Eggroll

The Decorator Who Knew Too Much

The Pajama Frame

Lover Come Hack

Apprehend Me No Flowers

Teacher's Threat

The Kill of It All

Love Me or Grieve Me

Please Don't Push Up the Daisies

The Glass Bottom Hoax

<u>Sylvia Stryker Outer Space Mysteries</u>

Murder on a Moon Trek

Scandal on a Moon Trek

Hijacked on a Moon Trek

Framed on a Moon Trek

Warped on a Moon Trek

<u>Material Witness Mysteries</u>

Suede to Rest

Crushed Velvet

Silk Stalkings

Tulle Death Do Us Part